Praise for
The Little Lion: A Hero in the Holocaust

Nancy Wright Beasley has written the poignant and haunting story of Laibale Gillman, an unassuming and ordinary teen-age boy who found strength, courage, and purpose when faced with the evils of Nazi Germany, which threatened the survival of his family and community. Stoked by the flames of her earlier book, *Izzy's Fire,* Nancy returns to her passion through *The Little Lion,* an in-depth character study of one young man's role in saving his people.
   — *Adriana Trigiani, bestselling author of* Big Stone Gap

During the Holocaust, Laibale Gillman, nicknamed "the little lion," was a hero to the people of Kovno Ghetto. He showed concern for others under the worst conditions and helped those weaker than him even when it put his life in danger. In telling Laibale's story, Nancy Wright Beasley, author of *Izzy's Fire,* once again shows the humanity that remains after everything else is taken away. *The Little Lion* is a wonderful book that I'm certain will be widely read.
   — *Martin Goldman, retired director of the Office of Survivor Affairs, United States Holocaust Memorial Museum*

This story keeps a reader constantly captivated and is a great choice for schools to use when teaching Holocaust education.
   — *Abigail Reasor, sophomore, Atlee High School*

Set in the Kovno ghetto during World War II and based on a true story, *The Little Lion* is the gripping tale of a Lithuanian boy's courage in the face of unspeakable Nazi horrors. The story sheds light on the risks Jews took to survive and is sure to spark discussion about the choices individuals make when pushed to the limit.
   — *A.B. Westrick, author of* Brotherhood

In today's frightening world, we must not forget that evil is still very real and very powerful. Stories of triumph in the face of evil must be told. *The Little Lion* is one of those stories.

— *Tom Width, artistic director, Swift Creek Mill Theatre, and director,* The Little Lion

Thanks to Swift Creek Mill Theatre, the timeless messages in Nancy Wright Beasley's historic novel will speak to a new generation of theatergoers. This story of a talented and heroic Jewish teenager protecting his family from German oppressors is inspiring and reminds us that, even in dire circumstances, the human spirit prevails.

— *Irene Ziegler, playwright,* The Little Lion

In the tradition of Aharon Appelfeld (*Baddenheim 1939 and The Age of Wonders*), *The Little Lion* exposes the insidiousness underlying the Holocaust cancer and emerges as an astounding testament to man's brutality toward his fellow man. A synthesis of despair, devastation, luck, hope, ingenuity, and triumph out of death, Beasley's witness-novel is a must-read for the Holocaust curriculum.

— *Melvin L. Macklin, PhD, assistant professor of English, Ferrum College*

The Little Lion shows the terrors of the Holocaust while being suitable for people of all ages. It is masterfully written and provides an excellent learning tool for anyone being exposed to the Holocaust.

— *Kaitlyn Sorensen, sophomore, Hanover High School*

In *The Little Lion*, Nancy Wright Beasley presents the Holocaust in simple language that will speak to adolescents and adults alike. A motorcycle race jumpstarts the book with action and sets the pace for the plot that reveals heart-wrenching historical correctness. Author of the powerful *Izzy's Fire: Finding Humanity in the Holocaust*, Nancy masterfully helps fill the void in Holocaust novels for the less-motivated reader. She wins the race in her first venture into historical fiction.

— *Paula Marshall, librarian, Chesterfield County Public Schools*

Laibale Gillman, a larger-than-life hero, will instantly grab the attention of middle school readers, especially the boys. Kudos to Mrs. Beasley for writing a book that will not only help students as well as adults learn about the Holocaust, but will also help them in making their own life decisions.

— *Rebecca Quesenberry, retired reading specialist*

In the prophet's dream the lion and the lamb dwell together in peace, but in Kovno Ghetto it took all the courage, skill, and imagination of a little lion—Laibale Gillman—to enable his family to endure. Nancy Wright Beasley has told his powerful story with sensitivity and skill. It makes for riveting reading and for a unique insight of life in Kaunas before and of daily life within the ghetto. I recommend it highly.

— *Michael Berenbaum, PhD, project director of the United States Holocaust Memorial Museum (1988-1993); author of* The World Must Know: The History of the Holocaust as Told in the United States Holocaust Memorial Museum

Also by the author

Izzy's Fire: Finding Humanity in the Holocaust
Reflections of a Purple Zebra: Essays of a Different Stripe

The
Little Lion

A Hero in the Holocaust

NANCY WRIGHT BEASLEY

POSIE PRESS
North Chesterfield, Virginia

Photos courtesy of Neil Bienstock, Israel Gillman,
Dr. Sara Pliamm, and the author.

This is a historical novel. While some characters are fictional, the story
is based on actual events that occurred and have been documented by
many of the individuals who are characters within the text; see author's
note. Some names, characters, places, and incidents either are a product
of the author's imagination or are used fictitiously.

Library of Congress Control Number: 2015949548
Beasley, Nancy Wright, 1945-
The little lion: a hero in the Holocaust / Nancy Wright Beasley — 1st. ed.

ISBN: 978-0-9861828-2-2 (p.bk.)
eISBN: 978-0-9861828-3-9

Manufactured in the United State of America on acid-free paper
Book design by Jason Smith
10987654321

*For Neilson J. November, a man whose
integrity and grace have been bastions
of strength for me. God has used Neil to
bless me immeasurably for two decades,
including underwriting my education
at Hollins University. Words
are inadequate to thank him.*

The Little Lion, *a young adult historical
novel, was submitted as my thesis to complete
an MFA in children's literature at Hollins
University in 2011. It was adapted for the
stage by Irene Ziegler and directed by Tom
Width at Swift Creek Mill Theatre in 2016.*

Acknowledgments

W here do I begin? There are countless people who need acknowledging, not only for their friendship but their unrelenting support over many years, especially Neil November, a dear friend and avid philanthropist to whom this book is dedicated.

I would be remiss not to mention the late Dr. J.D. Stahl. J.D. was my first, and I have to admit my favorite, professor at Hollins University while I was pursuing an MFA in children's literature. Anyone who met J.D., or took one of his classes, was instantly smitten by his vast knowledge, quiet demeanor, and endless dedication to the craft of writing for children and young adults. I learned through osmosis in J.D.'s classes. Although he agreed to be the critical analysis advisor for my thesis, sadly, leukemia claimed him before our work together could be completed. Dr. Tina Hanlon, an associate professor of English at Ferrum College and visiting professor at Hollins, graciously stepped in. Karen Adams, also a visiting professor at Hollins University and my thesis director, provided invaluable assistance. Over long months, Karen guided me with her insightful suggestions, until I reached the road leading to graduation. Mike and Shawna Christos spent many hours formatting the thesis and making sure it met specifications, while Diane Dillard, Inge Horowitz, Barbara Sadler, Gay Neale, as well as Rebecca Quesenberry and Howard Kellman provided endless encouragement.

Then, there was Neil Bienstock, who has helped me over many years by collecting stories and photographs from his grandfather, Israel Gillman. They have been a great team to work with. Also, Dr. Sara Gillman Pliamm has provided details of her parents' lives during World War II, as well as her own experience then. This book has developed over several years and became a reality because of their unflagging help. They also provided valuable family photographs, further authenticating the lives of their loved ones.

I fear to list other individuals, since I'd surely leave someone out. So many have given so unselfishly for such a long time. You know who you are, as you remain a very important part of my life. Please know that I will always be grateful for each phone call, card, visit, e-mail, bouquet of flowers and gift of chocolate, as well as the multiple times you advised me, either in person or across the miles. However, special thanks for many hours invested go to Carla Davis, who edited the manuscript, and to Jason Smith, who designed the interior of the book, as well as the cover. I'm very proud of their work and for all that each one of you has done to patiently bring *The Little Lion* to fruition.

To every one of you who helped me in any way, I will cite a phrase my precious mother, Beulah Mae Wright, often said to me during her last years: "Thanks for all the good help. You'll get your reward in heaven."

Table of Contents

Introduction 1
Chapter 1: The Race 7
Chapter 2: Laibale and Nese 15
Chapter 3: Joel Visits Germany. 23
Chapter 4: School Problems 31
Chapter 5: Pending Doom 39
Chapter 6: The Ghetto Formed. 45
Chapter 7: Leaving Home 53
Chapter 8: Entering Kovno Ghetto 61
Chapter 9: Unexpected Trouble. 69
Chapter 10: Resistance. 79
Chapter 11: Demokratu Square 85
Chapter 12: The Family Lives. 93
Chapter 13: Quiet Prevails. 99
Chapter 14: Escape Plan 107
Chapter 15: Laibale's Luck Changes 111
Chapter 16: Nese Needs Medicine. 115
Chapter 17: A Welcome Respite. 121
Chapter :18 Sheina and Sara. 125
Chapter 19: Father John 129
Chapter 20: Sara's Departure 133
Chapter 21: Surprise Search. 137
Chapter 22: Run For Life. 141
Chapter 23: Father Bruno 147
Chapter 24: A Stranger Helps. 151
Chapter 25: Unable To Hide 155
Author's Note. 159
Epilogue 161
Photos. 163
Book Club Questions 171
Standards of Learning/Virginia 173
Activities. 175
Recommended Resources. 177

Introduction

Laibale Gillman, the protagonist in *The Little Lion*, was an important character in *Izzy's Fire: Finding Humanity in the Holocaust.* In that book, which was published in 2005, I wrote of how Laibale was instrumental in helping several Jews escape Kovno Ghetto, including members of his own family.

What made Laibale's story so magnificent was how, as a teenager, he stood his ground against the Nazis, who perpetrated the most heinous crime against humanity the world has ever witnessed. While I was researching *Izzy's Fire*, I could scarcely believe the different stories that were relayed about Laibale, how he was able to come and go in Kovno Ghetto, like a vapor in the night. He wasn't of remarkable height, and he didn't have overly handsome features that would gain him any favors. What he did have was an innate mechanical ability to work on engines, especially motorcycle engines, which made him indispensable to the Nazis. Knowing that, Laibale stretched the limits of good sense as a Jew at that time, taking outlandish risks to escape the barbed wire fence surrounding the ghetto. Time and time again, drawing bravery from some unfathomable well, he made his way through the fence and, over a two-year period, returned bringing back food, medicine, and hope for the captives inside.

I used various memoirs and historical background information to write *Izzy's Fire*, which was nonfiction, but there was scant information about Laibale Gillman, save the few stories that had been handed down over the years. In order to write about him, I needed to fictionalize several characters and bring them to life to interact with Laibale and his family members. While they are fictional, they are based on individuals I've read about, many losing their lives in the ghettos, concentration camps, and faraway places like forests where they were forced to dig their own graves before being executed.

There is no way to tell how many young men, as well as some young women, like Laibale were sacrificed over the course of World War II. Because of the Holocaust, many Jewish families have been forced to live with the agony of not knowing the destination, or even the final resting place, for their loved ones. It is to those dear people, and to their children and grandchildren, that I hope to speak, letting them know that, although many of their loved ones lie silent in unmarked graves, their stories live on through the life and courage of Laibale Gillman.

It is my deepest hope that Laibale's bravery will be taken to heart by young adults and emulated as they face difficult choices in life. ~ Nancy Wright Beasley

But they that wait upon the Lord shall renew their strength;
They shall mount up with wings as eagles; they shall run
and not be weary; and they shall walk and not faint.
Isaiah 40:31 (KJV)

1

The Race

Laibale straddled his motorcycle and ground the dirt with his left foot. He and his friend Joel had arrived early at the starting line anticipating the race ahead. Several local school boys gathered nearby on their motorcycles.

"Look at the bastards," Laibale said under his breath. "They think they're going to win."

"Just seeing them makes me want to puke," Joel replied. "Don't worry. You're the best rider in Kaunas." He thumped his friend on the back.

"You mean in all of Lithuania, don't you?" Laibale asked, laughing.

Joel leaned over his own motorcycle and laughed, too. "I'm counting on you," he said. "You'll show 'em that Jews are just as good as anybody else. Nineteen thirty-eight will be remembered by everybody in Lithuania, especially here in Kaunas. You'll see to that."

Laibale smiled at his friend and then looked beyond Joel at the other seven riders. He knew them all and had already made a mental note of their bikes and how he could best them. He took deep breaths and tried to calm his heartbeat. Still, his confidence soared. He might be smaller than all of them but he knew he could beat them. No one was better than Laibale Gillman on a motorcycle. He had a reputation to maintain. He glanced over at Joel, who was right beside him. They had already made a pact. Whatever it took, one of them had to win.

The route and rules were well known, since the race was a much-anticipated annual event. The starting point was in the center of the market square in Kaunas where farmers gathered every Thursday to sell their wares. The racing route wound through the countryside, with the finish line deliberately set at the far end of the market square so more people could see it.

Engines rumbled, startling a flock of birds, which exploded into the air as motorcycles moved to the starting line. While Laibale waited to start, he fondly patted the side of his carefully restored Ariel. "We'll beat 'em, girl," he said. He glanced to the side and saw his mother standing near the front of the crowd. She was flanked on each side by his brothers, Israel, the middle son, and gentle Moshe, the oldest one who always settled arguments. Laibale knew his brothers would be there, but he was surprised to see his mother and overjoyed to see his grandmother perched on a kitchen stool that Moshe must have brought for her.

Laibale's mother had tried to talk him out of joining the race, saying it was too dangerous. She never understood what it was like to be a 15-year-old motorcycle racer. Still, she had managed to overcome her fears and smiled at him.

Laibale was surprised again when he recognized Peter Repsys waving at him with both arms way back in the crowd. Peter hadn't joined in the vicious taunting of the Jewish youths. Laibale and Peter had played together as children, becoming close friends when Laibale's mother taught Peter's mother how to sew. When they started school, though, their lives went different ways, as Laibale attended Hebrew school and Peter went to Catholic school. Still, they saw each other from time to time and shared a bond. There had never been a cross word between them.

The starter blew a whistle, then raised and dropped a flag. Laibale gunned his engine and was off, joining the group of teenage boys racing to lead the pack. Laibale wove in and out among the other riders, trying to stake a place at the front as they headed into the countryside. He concentrated hard on the route, dodging ruts that would destroy a tire and tried to remember what lay ahead. The competition thinned almost immediately, as two of the less experienced riders simply lost control of their motorcycles and went sprawling into the dirt.

Laibale leaned forward, his thoughts now racing in another direction. He couldn't believe he had ever been friends with the boys he was now determined to beat. In the last few months they had acted like Jews were maggots.

Remembering their hurtful comments made Laibale want to beat them even more. You'd think he and Joel had become lepers, the way they had been avoided by the other boys in town lately. When they did see him, there was always jeering involved. Laibale, who was just barely more than five feet tall, could be easily intimidated. At 15, he hadn't reached his last growth spurt, but Joel, a year older and nearly a foot taller, seemed fully grown. Laibale had been recently surrounded by a group of four or five bullies one day when Joel flailed into the group with fists flying and sent them scurrying. Joel was the perfect friend and Laibale was glad he had joined the race, too.

Laibale concentrated hard, watching one rider, trying to dodge a rock, cut in front of two others, which caused them all to lose control of their bikes. The pack of riders was suddenly down to four. Laibale managed to take the lead and held it through much of the remaining route. He looked over his shoulder from time to time, worried he might be overtaken.

"They're gaining on us," Joel screamed above the roar of the engines, as he managed to pass Laibale and take the lead just as they headed for the final stretch. They were getting close to the edge of the marketplace where the race would end.

Laibale glanced over his shoulder at the two closest riders, who were still a safe distance behind. Laughing from his advantage point, he turned forward again just in time to see Joel crash into a farmer's cart. Joel tumbled in one direction, while his bike slid through the dirt the opposite way and the engine stalled. Potatoes went everywhere.

Laibale dodged the runaway potatoes but caught a glimpse of Mr. Todras, one of the local farmers, shouting curses into the air. The engine on Laibale's bike screamed as he made a quick U-turn. He saw Joel trying to untangle himself from the cart as Mr. Todras stood over him, shouting. It was hopeless. Joel had lost his place. Laibale knew that going back wouldn't help Joel much and it would cost Laibale precious time.

Just as Laibale gunned his engine, Mr. Todras heaved potatoes toward him with both hands. "You'll pay for this!"

Laibale took off, certain that Joel would understand. The race had to be won. They had planned it for months. It was up to him now and nothing was going to keep him from winning. Not Joel's accident. Not potatoes. Not Mr. Todras' anger. Winning was all Laibale had thought about for weeks. He had to show those lousy locals, had to give them something to think about, especially since they had bragged about their new motorcycles and had made fun of his older, refurbished bike.

Laibale fleetingly thought about old Mr. Todras. Surely he had forgotten the race time; otherwise, he would never have been on Paneriu Street when the bikes came through. He came

into town about once a month to sell potatoes and other vegetables in order to feed his large family.

As he thought about the old man, Laibale hit a wet spot
and his bike slid out of control. By the time he had righted
himself, he had lost valuable time. The distance between
Laibale and the last two riders was now much shorter. George
Lietukis, the garage owner's son, was so close that Laibale
held his breath.

George roared past him. "What's the matter, Jew boy?" he
screamed. "Your big ears slowing you down?"

George's taunt made Laibale instantly angry. He quickly
adjusted the throttle, then opened it all the way and smiled
at its powerful response. When the bikes had been inspected,
no one had voiced an objection to Laibale's repairs, since they
really didn't even understand what he had done to the bike's
carburetor. Now, just as he'd planned, the revved-up engine
gave him an advantage. He pulled ahead of George in a spurt
and stayed in front for a few minutes. Suddenly his engine
sputtered, as it did sometimes when the gas mixture got low.
He wobbled and was almost thrown head over heels. In a
few seconds, though, the engine fired properly and he gunned
it again.

Laibale gained momentum as he pulled his knees closer to
the bike's chassis and leaned forward to cut down on wind
resistance. He pulled alongside George and saw the sweat-
soaked hair under his cap, his face set in an iron stare of
determination. The two neared the final turn, neck and neck.
Laibale was just barely aware of the people who lined the
street, elbowing each other so they could see.

When the motorcycles came into view, yells went up from
the crowd, now filled with women, children, townspeople,
and farmers. And there were others who had come from
neighboring areas just to see the race. Laibale glimpsed a small
bunch of his friends there as well, pushing to stay in front.

Near the finish line, Laibale streaked past one of the race officials and saw the man's mouth drop open. It was Mr. Lietukis,
George's father.

Suddenly it was over. The two motorcycles had been so
close that Laibale wasn't sure he had actually won. Then he
heard a bunch of girls chanting his name. "Lay-ba-lay, Lay-ba-
lay, Lay-ba-lay!" He even saw Rebekkah Weinstein, the prettiest
girl in school, waving and calling his name, stretching it out
for emphasis: "Lay-ba-lay, Lay-ba-lay, Lay-ba-lay!" Laibale
caught sight of George's father, Mr. Lietukis. Seeing the scowl
on Mr. Lietukis's face also confirmed Laibale's victory.

Laibale circled the marketplace and returned to face the
crowd. Just then he heard Mr. Lietukis holler, "Do you believe
that lousy Jew boy won?" His red face turned almost purple
as he glared at Laibale. He let out a string of curse words and
shook his fist at him.

Suddenly Laibale felt ten feet tall. He laughed to himself
as he dismounted and walked his bike through the thick crowd,
his friends closing ranks around him. When George's father
shouted, the farmers began making fun of him, which only
caused the red-faced man to curse louder. Suddenly, Laibale
felt a little sorry for George, even though he had been one of
the chief tormenters lately. Everyone knew that George's father
beat him for the slightest mistake. Laibale couldn't imagine
what might happen to him later.

"Laibale, you did it!" Joel shouted. "You did it!" He pushed
in close, grabbed Laibale in a bear hug, lifted him off the
ground, and pounded him on the back.

"Easy! Easy!" Laibale said, untangling his arms and pushing away. "I'm already out of breath."

Joel had to scream above the din. "I had my doubts, especially when old Todras got in the way, but you did it. You
showed those jackasses who was boss!" He raised himself up
like a peacock, as if he had won the race himself instead of

ending up in a pile of potatoes.

Shouts broke out among Laibale's friends. They nearly pulled his shirt off, lifting and hoisting him among themselves. His brothers, Moshe and Israel, pushed their way in to join the group, first pounding him on the back in excitement, then lending their hands so he could climb onto Joel's back. Laibale grabbed a handful of Joel's hair to keep from falling into the crowd. Their friends crushed together in jubilation and ran by a knot of men huddled in a circle. Laibale overheard one of the farmers disgusted with the outcome of his wager.

"Damned if I'm not afraid to go home. My wife will kill me for losing the market money," he said. "George's father is a mechanic, for God's sake. How could his boy lose to a Jew?"

Loud bickering continued as the men argued, either trying to renege on their bets or jostle a place in line to claim their earnings. Laibale had heard all week about how heavy wagers were being placed, mostly against him.

Then he caught sight of his mother. If he hadn't been on Joel's shoulders, he might have missed her in the back of the crowd. There she was, though, standing proudly next to Joel's mother in her plain gray dress, the one she wore almost every day. When their eyes met, she clapped her hands and jumped up and down. Laibale had never seen her so exuberant, not even when he won first place in the school's spelling competition a few years back.

He reveled in her excitement and waved his cap, glad for her attendance. She was always afraid he'd get hurt on his motorcycle. Laibale thought she was protective because he was her youngest child and the only one still at home. But she didn't understand that he knew he wouldn't get hurt, just as he knew he would win the race. His mother's mother, his special *bubbe*, on the other hand, had been confident that he would win and had quietly encouraged him. She was now standing proudly beside Laibale's mother, clapping her tiny hands and smiling broadly.

Just as Joel set him on the ground, a familiar voice said his name. He turned to see who was calling him.

It was Peter. "I'm proud of you, my friend," he said, extending his arms.

"Thanks, Peter," Laibale managed to get out, as Peter grabbed him in a bear hug. Laibale returned the hug, smiling up at his big friend.

"That was a helluva race!" Peter yelled. "You're the best motorcycle rider in Kaunas, hell, all of Lithuania!" Peter said, as he returned Laibale to the ground and thumped him on the back. Then Peter left, slipping quietly back into the crowd.

Laibale's friends surrounded him once more, jubilant in his success. Caught up in the excitement, Laibale knew it had been *his* race from the start. No one in Kaunas could get the best of him when it came to a motorcycle, either repairing one or racing one. It was a beautiful October day, and Laibale felt like he had just won the keys to a kingdom and he was the reigning king.

2

Laibale and Nese

L aibale got home late that night. He stopped a few steps from the front door, sensing that trouble awaited him. He could see through the window that his mother was still up. He watched her for a moment, her head bent over her mending by a dim lamp. The light from the lamp illuminated the auburn in her hair and Laibale realized how pretty she was. He wondered, although he had never had the courage to ask, why she never remarried or paid any attention to the several men who asked her out over the years. Laibale took a deep breath and opened the door.

"Hi, Mama. What are you doing up so late?" He hoped she would smile the way she had at the race.

But she didn't. She cut her eyes at Laibale, a dark look on her face. She dropped the mending into her lap.

"Do you know what time it is? Where have you been?"

"Celebrating, Mama, celebrating. I just couldn't get away. My friends are all so happy that I won."

A frown made the creases in her face stand out. "Well,

while you're celebrating, you might think about what it will cost me."

"What do you mean?" Laibale asked. "You didn't bet against me, did you?" He tried to hug her, hoping she would smile again.

She pulled away. "Stop it, Laibale. That's not funny. You won the race, all right. I'll give you that, but Mr. Todras is furious."

"Not with me. Joel's the one who crashed into his cart."

"Yes, but he thinks you're the ringleader. I had to promise to make two very nice blouses for his wife. Do you have any idea how long that will take me?"

"That's blackmail. That old grouch is just taking advantage of the situation. I'll make it up to you." He thought for a moment. "Don't you have some yard work Joel and I can do?"

"Work? Joel?" She practically snorted. "The only thing Joel works at is getting into trouble. Every time Joel is involved, there's a price to pay."

Laibale shrugged and took a deep breath, understanding that there was some truth in what she said. "And how were we to know that old Todras would have his cart in the way? Joel and I will do anything you want us to. I promise. Just tell me what you need and I'll take care of it. I can't believe that old crow made such a big deal over a few potatoes. He probably sold more than usual today, since there were so many people in town to see the race."

"Don't be disrespectful, Laibale," his mother said, her frown deepening. She turned toward the kitchen. "Mr. Todras works hard to grow his vegetables."

"Speaking of food, what's for supper?" Laibale crossed the room and raised the lid off a stewpot. "I think a winner at least deserves some hot potatoes and cabbage for his supper, don't you?"

"I guess so," his mother said, her face softening.

Laibale washed his hands and sat down. His mother wiped

off the red and white checkered oilcloth that covered the table as she always did and placed a bowl of steaming chicken soup, along with a heaping plate of vegetables, in front of him. His mouth watered as she sliced off a hunk of her wonderful *challah* bread. She passed the warm bread, along with the butter and a knife. Her face softened a little more, a smile playing around the corner of her lips. "I really was proud of you today, even though I worry about you and all the chances you take, you and that bike of yours."

Laibale spoke with his mouth full. "I wish you trusted me. I'm not a little boy anymore. I try not to get into trouble, although, like you said, that's hard to do around Joel. Sorry 'bout worrying you. I'll make you a promise, okay? I'll make you a *bubbe* three times before I'm 21."

The promise of grandchildren made his mother laugh outright, something she hadn't done in a while. "We shall see about that," she said in a gentle voice, as she placed the remaining food in the icebox, took off her apron, then handed Laibale another slice of bread and a jar of honey. "You'll need to get married first, I believe. But if you keep racing that motorcycle, you won't live to meet any girls."

"What do you mean?" Laibale sat up straight, pulled his short spine to its full height and stuck out his chest. "Did you see those girls in the marketplace today, clapping and shouting my name? In another year or two, when I'm ready to attend university, I'll have to run to get away from the *shiddach*."

"We'll see about that, too." His mother leaned over to give him a quick hug and rumple his hair, something else she hadn't done in a long time. She spoke in a tender voice. "Matchmakers may be in the future, but until then, Little Lion, eat your supper."

Laibale grinned at his mother, spreading honey on his bread. He caught a drip of it on his forefinger and licked it, making sure he got all the sweetness available. Laibale and his mother had formed a special bond between them. They had always talked together a lot, especially when Laibale was young. That's when his mother started calling him "Little Lion." Remembering this now, he couldn't help but smile, thinking of the first time she called him that. It was after he had saved his brother Moshe from a neighbor's dog. Although older by four years, Moshe was terrified of dogs and froze anytime one got near him.

Labile couldn't have been more than four or five when he heard Moshe yelling at the top of his lungs and discovered him crumpled beside the yard fence with a huge dog baring his teeth and snarling ferociously at him. Although terrified himself, Laibale picked up a yard rake and fended off the dog long enough to allow Moshe to escape into the house. For days afterwards, Laibale's mother retold the story, each time describing her youngest son as "the little lion" who protected his older brother. The day it happened, Laibale's mother put her arms around him and explained that he had just proved that size or age wasn't always important. She told him over and over how proud she was of his courage. That was the beginning of their long talks together. Nowadays, they still had long conversations when time permitted.

His mother sighed deeply, finally relaxed after the long day. "This will have to do for now," she said. She held up the little coat she had been making for Sara, Moshe's only child, her only grandchild. "That child is growing so fast, I'd better put a double hem in this," she said as she placed the garment in her sewing basket.

Laibale was always impressed with how carefully she kept everything arranged in that basket. Why, he'd seen her reach into it and retrieve the right color thread without even looking down. He wondered if her neatness had rubbed off on him. His penchant for orderliness had certainly come from somewhere.

His mother stood, stretching and yawning at the same time, as she walked over to pat Laibale on the shoulder.

"Don't stay up too late," she said. "It's been quite a day." She rubbed her eyes and walked down the hall toward her bedroom.

Laibale listened until his mother's footsteps faded into silence. She was such a good woman and deserved more than she'd gotten out of life. His father had divorced her long before and left her to fend for three boys. His two brothers moved out years ago. Moshe was married. Israel wasn't married but seemed to only have time for his girlfriend. Now there was just Laibale and his mother. It wasn't an easy thing for a seamstress to keep a household going, but somehow she managed. Laibale helped in any way he could. He chopped wood and carried water for neighbors and repaired mechanical things, all at a reasonable price.

He looked about the kitchen now, thankful for the familiar sight of the teapot his mother always placed on the stove for the following morning. Laibale took a deep breath, drawing in the familiar smell of the *challah* bread again. It was the first quiet time he'd had all day. He used a piece of crust to sop up the remainder of the chicken soup he loved so much, then gently scraped off the plate, placed it with the bowl in the sink, and ran water over them. He noticed the spigot was dripping again. His first repair job hadn't held. It might need another rubber washer.

Laibale thought maybe he and Joel could fix it together, although Joel barely knew the difference between a screwdriver and a wrench. Poor guy. He was more interested in girls than mechanics, so he usually just stood beside Laibale, waiting to be told which tool he needed.

Laibale took off his shoes and tiptoed down the hall. He paused for a moment and listened to his mother's easy breathing. He moved on to his room and slipped out of his clothes.

He decided to find Joel first thing in the morning and tell him they had to make it right with his mother. He sat on the side of the bed in the dark and relived the day, exhausted but wound up from all the excitement. The room was chilly, but he didn't get under the covers for a long time. Finally he lay down and pulled one of his mother's handmade quilts up to his chin. He smiled as he traced the nine diamond pattern with his hand, remembering the care his mother had taken in choosing blue and green cloth, his favorite colors.

He turned over on his stomach to give his sore rear end a break. He was used to riding a motorcycle, but today had been a lot rougher than usual. He hurt all over. When he shut his eyes, though, the only thing he could see was the scene when he crossed the finish line. Laibale relived every moment, burning it into his memory: the feel of the wind as it rushed through his hair, Joel ending up in a pile of potatoes, how the girls cheered, Peter's congratulations. He smiled again remembering how Rebekkah was shouting when he crossed the finish line. He even thought of Mr. Todras's threats and his overturned cart.

Laibale wondered if George's father was still mad about him losing the race. He thought it served Mr. Leitukis right, to be laughed at. Laibale remembered when he used to spend a lot of time at Mr. Leitukis's garage, along with George. Mr. Leitukis spent extra time explaining mechanics to Laibale, impressed with how quickly he caught on. Why, he had even loaned Laibale tools from time to time. But not anymore. Lately he had been curt even when Laibale tried to talk to him. Last week he didn't even speak when Laibale went to his shop. He just turned his back on him and talked to George, as if Laibale wasn't even there.

"I don't care what he or anyone else thought about me today," Laibale whispered quietly into the silent room. "No one could deny that I won. All that time I've spent working on my bike finally paid off."

Laibale straightened out the quilt, thinking again of how his mother had made it just for him. He closed his eyes and drew a deep breath. As he drifted off to sleep, he vowed to take on more responsibility and care for his mother, instead of the other way around. But he would think about that later. Tonight he only wanted to savor the sweetness of victory.

3

Joel Visits Germany

Laibale didn't see Joel for a couple of weeks. The talk in the neighborhood was that Joel's *bubbe* had died suddenly and that he had accompanied his mother to Germany to sit *shiva*, a time of observance to show respect for the dead. Laibale cried when he got the news. Joel's grandmother had always spoiled him when she visited, and treated him like another grandson. As bad as it was, though, her death allowed Joel and Laibale to be apart for a bit, which probably was a good thing. Based on his mother's reaction to the race, Laibale thought it was best to put some distance between himself and Joel for the time being.

Laibale's mother just stood quietly when he told her of the death. And then, the next day, Laibale knew the storm had passed when he returned from school and smelled his favorite dish. His mother's moods were reflected by the aromas coming from her kitchen. She always made *lochen kugel* when she was feeling generous, stirring it together in her big white-and-red enamel baking dish, which guaranteed leftovers for the next day.

Just as Laibale hurried into the kitchen, his mother pulled the steaming apple and noodle mixture from the oven. He carefully ran his finger along the mixing bowl, catching a drizzle of the mixture just before it dropped to the table, and tasted it. His mouth watered as he sat down at the table.

Although it was early afternoon and not time for supper, his mother dished out a serving for him. She chided him as he ate as fast as he could. "Slow down. You'll burn your mouth. Besides that, you won't even be able to taste it."

"Gotta hurry," Laibale said, his mouth full. "Save the rest for me, will you? I need to show the boys how to rebuild a carburetor."

"Don't you have school work to do?"

"Yes, but not much. I can do it before bedtime." He pushed his chair back and wiped his mouth.

"It won't be long until supper. Just make sure you're home on time." His mother arched an eyebrow.

"I promise." Laibale kissed her cheek and ran out the door. He wanted to get to the shed before anyone else arrived so he could get the tools lined up. He wondered if Joel would be back from Germany.

Joel was already there, pacing outside the shed.

"Hey Joel, I'm sorry about your *bubbe*," Laibale said as he unlocked the door. "I didn't hear about her until after you left."

Joel nodded. "Mama was in a big hurry to get there," he said. "But she was in just as big a hurry to leave. I've never been so glad to get home. You won't believe what I saw."

"Hand me those tools, starting with the socket wrench," Laibale said, cutting him off. "I need to get things set up. We can talk while I get ready."

Joel gave Laibale the wrong tool.

"Not that one, *yutz*. The one on the end. How many times do I have to show you which one is the socket wrench?"

Joel faced him. "Laibale, listen!" he said, his voice rising almost to a shout.

"Okay, okay," Laibale said. He wiped his hands with a rag and turned to Joel, giving him his full attention. "You don't have to holler."

Joel stepped closer to Laibale and spoke quietly and quickly.

"I saw something so terrible." Joel paused and gulped.

"Like what?"

"The Nazis. They were burning buildings."

"Burning buildings? What are you talking about?"

"I'm talking about synagogues, schools, and stores being set on fire and people being beaten and arrested," Joel said, his eyes growing wider, as he wrung his hands. He was clearly upset.

"Come on, Joel. That's impossible."

"I saw it with my own eyes," Joel insisted, the pitch in his voice rising. He began to pace, making fists as he walked. "The rabbis were all running around, trying to save the Torahs. The Brown Shirts just pushed them out of the way, even laughed as the Torahs were being stomped into the ground. It was terrible!"

"That's crazy, Joel, you're not making any sense. Why would anyone do that?"

"I don't know, but I saw it, I tell you, just as Mama and I got into town. People were running everywhere, screaming. There were lots of German soldiers, but they just stood there and watched it all happen. Some of the local men were beating the shop owners with hoes and mattocks. I saw one old rabbi with only half a beard."

"What?"

"His face was bleeding terribly. His beard had been yanked out." Joel was shivering. "Mama and I hid in an alley behind some old sauerkraut kegs. We managed to get to Uncle Harold's house after dark."

Laibale's mind raced. What Joel said was beyond belief. How could Laibale doubt his best friend, someone he saw almost every day? They stuck so close to each other that their mothers teased them about being twins. They had been lifelong friends and were inseparable. Laibale had even gone with Joel to visit Joel's Uncle Harold and Aunt Inge several times. They always treated Laibale like part of the family.

"We rushed inside Uncle Harold's house," Joel continued. "He shoved us into the kitchen pantry and told us to stay quiet."

"Why were you hiding? Your uncle is a huge man. I don't understand."

"At first I couldn't hear." Joel lowered his voice to a whisper. "I cracked the door and listened to Uncle Harold and some of his neighbors talking about the ransacking. Mr. Meth was crying. I could barely make out what he had said. His brother and nephews were dragged out of their homes and beaten. His nephews were arrested and taken away. Mr. Meth's brother lost so much blood he might not live. Nobody dared take him to a doctor."

Laibale's heart pounded. "What did your uncle do? I can't imagine him being afraid of anything."

"He was plenty scared. Thank God my uncle was sitting *shiva*. He wasn't in his leather shop when the hoodlums started looting. It was burned to the ground. Uncle Harold said it's happening all over. They're after all the Jews. Everybody is staying behind locked doors. They're big shots now, those dirty Nazis. They hate us. Worse yet, they want to stamp us out."

"Why"

"Uncle Harold says they think Jews are dirty, like vermin or lice. My uncle said it had a lot to do with money, too."

Laibale managed to calm Joel down just as the other three boys arrived. Joel began retelling the story to them, adding more details the second time. Joel was becoming more upset.

The other boys did, too, as they listened.

"Let's call this off for today," Laibale interrupted. "Nobody will be able to concentrate. We'll get together tomorrow, same time."

Laibale left Joel huddled with the others and headed for home. It was a chilly November day, yet he hadn't worn a coat. He wasn't often cold. He was the kind of person who always looked forward to the first snowfall every year. Sometimes he rode his motorcycle during the winter months wearing only short-sleeved shirts. But today was different. Laibale suddenly felt his teeth chatter. He pulled up his shirt collar and stuffed his hands inside his pants pockets. The wind whipping around him bit at his fingers. He couldn't feel his toes. The chill deepened when rain began to fall. Within minutes he was soaked. He leaned his head into the rain and quickened his pace.

He was puzzled by Joel. He wondered if his friend had heard things right. Still, last month one of the rabbis and his assistant had left Kaunas and neither had returned. The men's disappearance and Joel's stories made no sense. Who would kidnap or torture rabbis? After all, rabbis were always considered some of the most revered men in the neighborhood. Laibale hoped Joel was somehow mistaken.

Daylight slipped away just as Laibale got home. He left his wet shoes by the door, then went and changed his clothes in a hurry. As he huddled by the warm stove in the kitchen, he decided to tell Joel's story to his mother. She listened politely and then turned back to cooking without saying a word. Her silence aggravated him.

"Mama, I know you have your doubts about Joel, but he said the Nazis are on the move. He thinks we're all doomed. He said Jews should try to escape."

His mother peeled a potato as if she was angry at it. Finally, she rinsed her hands and put them on her hips. "It's just Joel trying to stir up mischief."

"I believe him. He saw stores and a synagogue wrecked and...." He paused, took a deep breath, and tried to keep his voice calm as he spoke in his friend's defense.

"Even our sacred Torahs were being burned. Joel saw it all with his own eyes, I tell you."

"Nonsense," his mother scoffed. "Joel isn't happy unless he's in the middle of some uproar. Remember when he almost started a fight between two men over some tall tale?"

"This is different," Laibale insisted quietly.

"Laibale, Laibale," his mother said, wiping her hands on her apron. "Are you *meshuggah?* Only a crazy person would believe that story. Use your brain. Does it make sense that shops and synagogues are being burned and Jews are being beaten like dogs in the street? Would human beings treat other humans like that? No! Now take Joel's nonsense and go away."

Laibale was confused. How could Joel believe those things, even if he said he had witnessed them? Nothing like that had ever happened before. Laibale wondered if Joel was just playing a joke and would let him in on it the next day. After all, Joel had always been one to exaggerate. But he had been so upset. That seemed real. Even though Laibale tried, he couldn't shake off the dark feelings that made his stomach queasy.

Everyone had downplayed similar stories that had been spreading lately. They were terrified of Hitler, especially since he was always on the radio, always screaming about his political plans.

Laibale's mother turned her back to him, her silent signal that the conversation was over. The longer he stayed in the kitchen, the more agitated he became. It would be a while before supper was ready. He walked to the door and wrapped a scarf around his neck.

"Give a holler when supper's ready, okay?" Laibale said. "I'm going to walk outside for a little while." His mother just nodded without looking at him. He went back into the street thankful the rain had stopped.

Laibale found the group of men who gathered each evening by an open fire barrel. They smoked their cigarettes and held their hands over the flames, usually glad to be finished with another day's work. Today, though, the air was full of tension. Laibale arrived just in time to hear one of the neighborhood men, whom Laibale knew, describe his trip to Vilnius, a bordering city.

"I went into the city to get some barrel rings," the man said. "When I got close to Emmanuel's shop, I saw that all the windows had been broken. The building was empty. It had a huge yellow star painted on the front and the words 'Closed permanently.'"

Another man spoke up. "Well, maybe Emmanuel did it himself," he said. "You know how he is. He's always looking for ways to make money so he can go out of business and stay home with that new wife of his. Why, one day he even said he'd burn the place down for the insurance money if he thought he could get away with it."

The first man nodded. "Yes, I've heard him say stupid things as well, but this was different. On another street, all the Jewish shops had been boarded up and were vacant."

"Well, maybe Emmanuel got them all to go out of business to drive up the prices. Who knows what he would do?"

A door slammed nearby, which made the two men jump. One of the wives called out that supper was ready, and the group began to break up. Still, a few men stayed clustered together. Laibale, not wanting to be alone, joined them, shivering at the similarity between the men's stories and Joel's. No one seemed to take them seriously, though. A few men even laughed.

But Laibale found no humor in the stories. He remembered Joel's eyes and trembling hands. These men were no strangers, but men he knew and trusted. Like Joel, they seemed frantic in their desire to be taken seriously. While Joel was young, these men were not. Still, age hadn't bought them respect. At the end they were scoffed at, too.

A moment later, Laibale heard his mother call him to supper. He said goodbye and walked home, more convinced than ever that Joel was telling the truth. Even though he knew his mother couldn't hear him, Laibale muttered, "No, Mama. I'm not *meshuggah*. I am using my brain, and it tells me that something is definitely wrong."

4

School Problems

Laibale went to school the next morning. He tried not to think about what he had heard the night before. He thought instead about Rebekkah Weinstein and hoped he would see her. He paused just outside the school door. Lately he had to stir up his courage before entering the building. He took a minute to straighten his collar and inspect his clothes. He was tightening his belt when Joel walked up.

"Why are you acting so prissy?" Joel said in the sarcastic way he usually saved for the other boys. "You've acted more like a girl than a boy lately."

Laibale shrugged. "Just checking to make sure my shirttail was tucked in. Mr. Brown has been hammering me about that lately."

"Since when did our principal start to check shirttails?"

"Well, there's been a lot of talk about uniforms. If we don't start being neater, we may be forced to wear them, and my mother can't afford uniforms."

Laibale glanced around.

"She's not here," Joel said. "Give up."

"What do you mean?" Laibale asked innocently, still looking over Joel's shoulder.

"Rebekkah Weinstein. I know you're sweet on her."

Laibale laughed. "I just wanted to tell her something," he said, turning his face so Joel couldn't see that he was blushing. Laibale hoped to talk privately with Rebekkah in the hall before classes began. If he didn't find the courage to approach her soon, spring would turn into summer and he would lose the chance. Her family always went to the seaside during the summer months.

"C'mon, Laibale. We've got just enough time to grab a smoke before class."

"Have you been stealing your mother's cigarettes again?"

"A few here or there won't matter. She smokes so much, she'll never miss them."

"Mama said she'd kill me if I ever started smoking, and I believe her. Besides that, she can smell tobacco a mile away. Don't you know that smoking stunts your growth?"

"Looks like you've been smoking for a long time already." Joel laughed out loud and patted the top of his short friend's head. Laibale knocked his hand away, but Joel landed a punch on Laibale's shoulder. Laibale composed himself again and stepped inside the building. He opened a school book and leaned against one of the main walls. He stood that way for a long time. It appeared hopeless. No matter how much he polished his shoes or how well he dressed, Rebekkah didn't seem to notice him. She didn't know how he shut his eyes in bed every night and wished he could touch her silky blond hair. Sometimes she wore braids and wrapped them around her head like a halo, exposing her creamy porcelain neck. When she turned her head just right, Laibale could see her lips. It made him think about kissing her.

Laibale pretended to concentrate while he looked over the edge of his book. He craned his neck and looked up and down the hall again. He could pick Rebekkah out in a crowd. She seemed almost magical and, well, not so Jewish. Her blue eyes reminded him of the marbles he used to play with, the ones he kept in a glass pint jar on his dresser. Every so often, he'd take them out and hold them against the window while he thought about her eyes. When the sun hit the marbles just right, they'd flash back at Laibale as if Rebekkah had winked. One time he swore he heard her giggle at him with affection.

He knew that was pure daydream, but he couldn't stop thinking of how close his mother would be to Rebekkah soon, as she had been asked to make Rebekkah's new spring dresses. While his mother had rejoiced over the money she'd make, Laibale imagined how her hands might touch Rebekkah's body as she took the measurements around her breasts and hips. Thinking about Rebekkah took his mind off everything. His imagination ran wild as he stood motionless against the wall.

Joel punched Laibale on the shoulder again, bringing him back to reality. "You'd better hurry, short stuff, or we'll both be tardy."

"Race you to class," Laibale called over his shoulder. He managed to get into his seat ahead of Joel. Both of them were out of breath. Laibale glanced to the front of the class to see if their teacher had noticed. But, instead of Mrs. Jacobs, it was Mr. Brown, the principal who faced them.

Joel leaned over. "Uh oh. This means trouble. What do you think Mr. Brown's doing here?" He spoke in a low voice. "He's usually too hung over to make it to school too early."

"I don't know. Maybe he's trying to get in some licks before spring break. Be quiet so we can hear."

Mr. Brown stood before them, waiting for the class to settle down. Mrs. Jacobs stood tensely in the back of the room, also waiting.

Mr. Brown rapped on the teacher's desk. His knuckles were white as he gripped a ruler. "Students. Students. Come to order. I need everyone's attention. Please come to order." Joel whispered from behind his hand. "Yeah, yeah, somebody has probably written on the walls again."

"I don't know," Laibale whispered back. "He looks strange."

Mr. Brown cleared his throat. "There has been a terrible accident." He cleared his throat again, took a deep breath, and spoke louder and higher.

"Two of our beloved teachers, Mr. Heimlich and Mr. Horowitz, were killed in a car wreck last night."

All the air seemed to be sucked out of the room. Mr. Brown paused so his words could sink in. Then the classroom erupted so loudly he had to bang the desk repeatedly for silence. He began again. "There will be no Hebrew classes this afternoon. There will be a staff meeting instead. By tomorrow you'll be reassigned to other classrooms.

The students murmured among themselves. "This is a terrible loss for all of us," Mr. Brown said, looking out over the stunned students. His voice broke. "As you know, Mr. Heimlich and Mr. Horowitz were the best of friends. There will be a joint service tomorrow at 4 p.m. at the Kaunas Synagogue. Their families will be sitting *shiva* for the next seven days. I hope you all will pay your respects."

Mr. Brown excused himself and left for the next classroom. The students sat in stunned silence. Mrs. Jacobs walked up to the desk, straightening her skirt. She made a few announcements, but nobody was listening. Finally, her face crumpling into tears, she sat down and put her head in her hands for a few minutes. Seeing their teacher so distressed caused the students to become quiet and respectful. One of the girls offered Mrs. Jacobs a handkerchief and returned to her seat. The teacher blew her nose, breathed deeply a couple of times, and squared her shoulders before standing up.

"Students, I think it would be very beneficial for you to consider what effect these two teachers have had on your lives. I want each of you to write an essay about a special memory you have of Mr. Horowitz or Mr. Heimlich. They have been Hebrew teachers here for about twenty years and I know that each of you have had classes they've taught. You will be adults, perhaps with children of your own, before you truly understand what they have done for you." She paused for a moment, took another deep breath, and started again.

"The paper doesn't have to be long, but it does have to be an honest representation of your experiences. I want you to finish the paper in this class period. I'll put them in a binder tonight. Take a few minutes and talk among yourselves and decide on someone to be a class representative. That person can present them to Mrs. Horowitz and Mrs. Heimlich after their services. I believe that would mean a great deal to them in the days ahead."

The classroom remained quiet, except for the scribbling of pencils. An occasional sigh or sniffle escaped from some of the girls. Finally, the class was over. Mrs. Jacobs accepted the papers as she watched the students file out. For the first time since Laibale could remember, no one was talking. No one shoved or pushed to get into the hallway. Many students were crying and some teachers, too. Little groups of people stood outside the classroom doors, some of them hugging each other.

Joel caught up with Laibale. "Didn't I tell you that something was wrong? Didn't I? Maybe you'll believe me now. I can't believe Heimlich and Horowitz were just snuffed out. I thought those two old birds would live forever."

Laibale nodded. "Yeah, I guess you're right. Something seems too strange about it, especially when they were both fine yesterday. I can't believe they died in a car wreck. Mr. Heimlich always drove like a turtle, just like he walked. He got after me all the time for riding my bike so fast. Mr.

Brown looked like a scared rabbit. Did you see how pale he was?"

"Yeah, he looked kind of strange, now that you mention it."

"Well, I've got to get to the library before class," Laibale said.

"Right. Well, if you walk slowly, maybe you'll run into Rebekkkkkahhhh on your way."

Laibale had tried to keep his thoughts about Rebekkah secret from everybody, especially Joel. He knew that Joel would make fun of him, or worse, tell the other boys, and then they would all poke fun at him. Sometimes Joel had a cruel streak, but he usually spared Laibale. How could they understand that he simply dreamed of just taking a walk with Rebekkah or seeing her during *Shabbat* services on Friday night? That's all it could ever be, though, a dream. She wouldn't be allowed to associate with him. Her family expected her to marry high class, maybe an attorney or a rabbi, like her older sister had. Even though Rebekkah and Laibale attended the same school, they lived in such different worlds: she was a doctor's daughter and he was the son of a seamstress.

He turned his thoughts toward his next class. Mr. Brown might as well have dismissed school. Nobody was going to learn anything this day. Every class buzzed about the accident. Some teachers were more affected than students. Mrs. Lowry sat at her desk with her head in her hands, while the students milled around the class and comforted each other. One girl even fainted in the hall and caused a stir.

Just as Laibale walked into their next class, he caught Israel November's eye. Israel wedged his big frame into a seat that belonged to someone else. He leaned over and whispered, "Laibale, did you hear what really happened to Mr. Heimlich and Mr. Horowitz last night?"

"Mr. Brown said they were in a car wreck."

"No such thing," Israel fired back. He leaned closer. "They were beaten to death."

Laibale felt a chill rush over his body. His lungs tightened and it was hard to breathe. "*Murdered*?" he finally managed to say. "Who told you that?"

"Never mind. It was a reliable source. I've been sworn to secrecy." Israel looked over his shoulder and slid even closer. Their shoulders touched.

"It happened all right, and after they killed them, they stuffed their bodies inside the car and tried to fake an accident." Israel drew in a breath. "And, somebody we know did it."

Laibale's mouth fell open. "What? I don't know any murderers."

"You'll be surprised when you find out," Israel said. "Can't talk right now. Just don't say I didn't try to tell you." He pulled away from Laibale.

"I don't believe you."

"You'll be sorry you ever doubted me." With a smug look on his face, Israel freed himself from the desk, rose, and took his proper seat.

Laibale felt sick to his stomach. It seemed that, no matter which way he turned lately, something was always wrong.

5

Pending Doom

As Laibale waited for his literature class to begin, he rested his head on his desk and concentrated on Rebekkah, hoping to block out what Israel had just told him. Either thought was torture right now, but Rebekkah was certainly the more pleasant one. Laibale knew it would only be a matter of minutes before Mrs. Rose made her grand entrance and all eyes would have to be on her for the rest of the class period.

If anyone had the right name, it was Mrs. Rose. She blushed so often that her cheeks were always rosy. She wore a sort of lavender pink lipstick, which made her face seem even redder. She was a little pudgy, too, and when her face flushed she reminded Laibale of one of those little Hummel figurines that his mother had wanted ever since she saw one a few years ago in Germany.

Mrs. Rose had always been one of Laibale's favorite teachers. She was very understanding, as she taught different grade levels and had known most of the students for years. She always had a lot of patience with serious students. Joel, who certainly couldn't be considered serious, made fun of her and said she was prissy. He thought it funny that she checked her lipstick in a little mirror several times a class period, especially when she knew Mr. Brown was coming in to make an announcement. Joel stole the mirror out of her desk drawer one day, but he put it back when Laibale threatened to tell Mr. Brown what he had done.

Mrs. Rose came into the room dabbing her nose with a handkerchief, like she had been crying. Laibale wondered if she had heard the two teachers were murdered, too, because she was so red she looked like she was on fire. She fanned herself, like she always did, but it didn't seem to cool her off.

Usually Mrs. Rose quietly gave directions, telling the students to sit down and get out their books, even before the class started. Today, though, she didn't take her eyes off the homework papers everyone had been laying on her desk as they filed into class. She just kept sorting the homework into piles and then rearranging them like she didn't really want to speak to anyone, until Rebekkah walked in.

"Good morning, Rebekkah," Mrs. Rose said. From the corner of his eye, Laibale watched Rebekkah come into the room. Even though Laibale had seen her many times, her beauty always took him by surprise.

"Good morning," Rebekkah answered softly, as she handed her homework to Mrs. Rose. She walked by Laibale to her assigned seat. Her closeness made him feel warm, and he suddenly wished he could borrow Mrs. Rose's fan. Rebekkah had a way of gliding instead of walking. Before sitting down, she used her hands to tuck her skirt under her knees, and halfway knelt beside her desk, balancing herself on her toes. She carefully arranged her books underneath her desk, putting the big ones on the bottom, lining them up according to size so they'd be even on all sides and wouldn't topple over.

Rebekkah's books reminded Laibale of Mr. Fine's garden, the one he and Joel passed each day walking to school. Mr. Fine's tomatoes looked like he had used a ruler to set them out, the plants perfectly lined up and growing like soldiers marching across the field.

"Clear your desks," Mrs. Rose finally said, bringing the class to order as the last two boys rushed into the room, bumping each other as they came through the door. Laibale watched Rebekkah. She followed the same routine every day. Sometimes, though, depending on which way she leaned over her books, Laibale could see down her blouse. He knew he wasn't supposed to look, and it made him nervous, but he did it anyway. As Rebekkah finally slid into her seat, Laibale wondered about her. What was her favorite color? Could she dance? What did she dream about?

"We're going to do a different assignment today," Mrs. Rose announced.

Laibale heard Mrs. Rose, but it sounded like she was a thousand miles away. He tried to imagine what it would be like to take Rebekkah to a movie. Their town was so small they could easily walk to the theater and back before dark, especially in the spring. Besides, Rebekkah's father would never let her ride on a motorcycle. Sometimes Laibale broke out in a sweat just thinking about what it might be like to have her sitting behind him on the bike, snuggled up to his back, and holding onto his waist with her tiny hands, her golden hair blowing in the breeze. Laibale knew that would never be, especially since the men and women even sat separately during synagogue services, but he liked to dream just the same.

Mrs. Rose popped a ruler on the top of her desk, startling everyone in the room. She raised her voice, too, which she never had done. The one thing the students could count on was that Mrs. Rose never changed routines. She was so predictable that they could tell which day of the week it was by what she wore: blue dress on Monday, white blouse and black skirt on Tuesday, a gray suit for Wednesday and Thursday, and the blue dress again on Friday. The only thing that changed was her shoes, either black pumps or brown lace-ups. Sometimes Joel and Laibale bet each other which pair of shoes she would wear with which dress. Laibale usually won. Every student knew Mrs. Rose was just marking time until she retired. As long as they got to class on time, turned in their homework assignment, and didn't fall out of the chair while she was talking, they could count on a passing grade.

"I said come to attention, class. We're going to do a different kind of assignment today." She spoke in a strange, tight-lipped voice. "I thought we might use the newspaper for our lesson."

Newspaper? Laibale suddenly jerked up straight in his desk, wondering what would make her say such a thing.

She began in a quiet voice, looking down at the newspaper in her hands. "I've been reading some disturbing public notices in the paper lately. Can anyone tell me the purpose of public notices?" She finally looked at the class as a group. Laibale believed he knew the answer but decided to wait and see what happened. Maybe this would be the most interesting literature class all year.

Israel crouched down in his desk, trying to avoid Mrs. Rose's look.

"Israel November, can you tell us the answer?"

"Well, not exactly, Mrs. Rose. I don't read the paper very much." He looked at his fingernails instead of directly at Mrs. Rose.

"I see," Mrs. Rose said, taking off her wire-rimmed glasses and fanning herself as she looked at the class again. "Do I have any volunteers?" No one was surprised when Rebekkah's hand shot up first. She was an excellent student. "All right, Rebekkah, what is the answer?"

"A public notice is a special announcement and it's supposed to be for everyone's benefit," Rebekkah said. She shrugged off her green flowered sweater and draped it over the back of her desk chair, hiding the initials someone had carved into the back of it years ago. Laibale concentrated on Rebekkah's sweater and wondered what kind of real flowers she liked.

"Where would you expect to see a public notice, Laibale?" Mrs. Rose asked. "Laibale Gillman, are you listening?" Mrs. Rose's voice rose.

Laibale faltered, suddenly realizing Mrs. Rose was talking to him. His face was hot and he knew it was as red as hers.

He stammered. "Well, uh, public notices are usually nailed on the side of buildings, like courthouses," he said. "Sometimes they're tacked up in the synagogue, along with the bar mitzvah invitations, right beside the rabbi's office."

"And would you consider a bar mitzvah invitation a public notice?" Mrs. Rose asked, still looking directly at Laibale, adding to his discomfort.

"Well, uh, I don't know that I ever thought about it." Desperate for an answer, he added, "That depends on whether you're Jewish or not, I suppose."

Mrs. Rose sighed, and some of the students snickered. Laibale wondered: Was Rebekkah smiling at him?

"Bar mitzvahs are considered public notices in my synagogue," Rebekkah said in a quiet voice that sent shivers down Laibale's spine. "They are an open invitation for any synagogue member who wants to come to the celebration."

"Very well then, Rebekkah. I suppose you have a point. Now for today's lesson, I'm going to read a public notice that was in a newspaper in Munich recently. My sister was visiting me last night and she brought it with her." Mrs. Rose shuffled the newspaper but couldn't find the announcement immediately. She looked up to quiet the class just as Rebekkah raised her hand and asked if she could sharpen her pencil. Watching Rebekkah walk across the room set off Laibale's thoughts again. It was like seeing the latest model of a motorcycle and knowing he would never own it or even touch it, a dream out of reach and only to be admired from a distance.

"Here, I found it," Mrs. Rose said. She walked down the aisle and stood beside Laibale, giving him a stare that made him sit up and pay close attention. As she read, Laibale could see the announcement. It had thick black headlines across the page.

ATTENTION GERMAN CITIZENS!

IT IS FORBIDDEN TO BUY MERCHANDISE FROM JEWS. NO JEWS WILL BE ALLOWED TO BUY FROM GENTILES. ANY JEWS SHOPPING IN GENTILE STORES WILL BE IMMEDIATELY ARRESTED.

Laibale didn't feel hot any more. Now he felt cold to the bone.

6

The Ghetto Formed

Every day neighbors ran to find a newspaper, looking to see what new announcements had been published. Mr. Howenstein, who lived next door to the Gillmans, always took his paper over to Laibale's mother after he read it. He had been doing that for years, saving her the money for delivery. Laibale tried to wait for him before leaving for school but sometimes Mr. Howenstein was late, which left Laibale dependent upon Joel for the news when he got to school.

Public notices, most of them pertaining to Jews, began appearing almost daily on the side of the court building near the center of town. Crowds gathered each day to read what new restrictions had been placed on the Jews. The announcements were also read over the radio each morning.

The list grew so fast and the restrictions became so numerous that sometimes Laibale's head hurt just trying to remember what was forbidden. The Nuremberg Laws, passed in 1935 in Germany, were now spreading throughout Europe. Suddenly Jews weren't allowed to walk on the sidewalks, go to public parks, or attend movie theaters or public schools. All but one of the Hebrew schools, the one Joel and Laibale attended, had already been shut down. Most students were staying at home. The *yeshivas*, where Europe's most learned rabbis were schooled, had been forced to turn out all their rabbinical students after the night in Germany, where Joel witnessed the riots and pillaging. People now called that night *Kristallnacht*, or "The Night of Broken Glass."

Most Jews, especially the older ones, were afraid to leave their homes except for bare necessities. So many businesses had been closed down by restrictions that it was nearly impossible to get daily supplies, especially butter and sugar. The shops now either stood vacant or were run by government appointees. Some Jews were even forbidden to buy items from the inventory they once owned themselves. There were no plans to rebuild the shops that had been destroyed.

Some restrictions affected Gentiles as well. They were now forbidden to make purchases at the few remaining Jewish shops or partake in any Jewish business or service. Most of the Jewish shop owners were forced to sell their businesses for paltry sums to Gentiles. The elderly Jews, who simply feared to resist, had their possessions confiscated. There was such despair that people were practically giving away their homes and furniture for a few dollars and leaving the country or running to seek refuge with relatives in other towns. Laibale even heard of one family that traded their fine home and a very expensive car for a single railroad ticket so the father could get out of Lithuania.

Every day, it seemed, there was a report of another suicide. Two brothers who both worked for banks in Kaunas, hanged themselves on the same day. After that happened, some of the older men decided they would start visiting the families that were hardest hit by the restrictions. It seemed to help, as there were no more suicides right away. Laibale's mother, though, over the past hard year, was fortunate in her own business. Her easy-going manner and good rapport with her customers was paying off. Now that specialty shops were closed, the demand for her fine needlework had actually increased. Many of her longtime customers defied the restrictions about doing business with Jews and continued to secretly request her work. She had to be discreet about delivering the clothes and accepting payment, though, since it was so difficult to tell who could be trusted. Still, people were having babies that needed clothes, and Laibale and his mother needed to eat. So she kept working despite the risk. Laibale even managed to make a bit of money from motorcycle repair, doing most of it at night and always with Joel as a lookout. They never went anywhere alone. They always accompanied their mothers as well.

One day, delivering repaired vestments with his mother to the local priest, Laibale decided to ask for a favor. Father John had known them all their lives. He had tried to help Laibale's mother at first, after the divorce, asking her to sew vestments for him and altar cloths for the church. He had a deep appreciation for the quality of her work. Over the years they had become friends, and Laibale's mother often took him some of her wonderful *challah* bread and homemade preserves when she delivered his order. She always shared what she had, especially if someone lived alone. It was her way of performing *tzedakah*, helping those in need. As for the priest, Laibale's mother often told Laibale that Father John needed someone to look after him, since he lived alone. She and Father John often had tea together and discussed religion, something that was almost unheard of between a Catholic and a Jew.

On this trip, though, there wasn't time for that. Laibale waited until their visit was coming to an end and asked if he could speak to Father John in private. Laibale's mother raised an eyebrow at the strange request but sat down again.

Once they were standing outside on the porch, Father John asked, "Yes, Laibale? What's so important that your mother can't hear?"

"Well, Father, I've been thinking about our life. It's getting so very hard for Jews now."

"Yes, that's so, Laibale. It's not just in Lithuania, but all over Europe. Still, what's troubling you?"

Laibale's heart started beating hard. Suddenly he was afraid that his voice would quiver. He cleared his throat. "I know you have a great deal of respect for my mother, or I would never ask you for a favor."

"You know I'll help you if I can, but it's dangerous for us to be out here together. You know everyone is being watched."

Laibale cleared his throat once more and spoke quietly. "Yes, well, I wondered if, perhaps, you might consider allowing me to hide my motorcycle here somewhere at the church or maybe in the cemetery," he said, rushing to get it all out. "I could have Peter Repsys bring it one night after dark. I gave my bike to him for safekeeping. Since he attends your church, it wouldn't seem strange for him to come to see you. Perhaps you know a good place where it would be safe."

Father John gasped a little and placed both hands near his temples, like he had a sudden headache.

"I don't know, Laibale," he said, lowering his voice and stepping close. "That's putting me in a terribly awkward position. What if the officials start asking questions? They'd think it's mighty peculiar that I suddenly acquired a motorcycle. After all, I'm a bit old to be riding a motorcycle and I already have a car. And, what about Peter? He's a fine boy, but are you sure he can be trusted with this kind of information?"

"Yes, Father. Peter has stuck up for me on more than one occasion. He said that he felt terrible about all the restrictions being placed on the Jews and that he would do anything he could to help me."

"Well, my son, that was then and this is now. Things have changed considerably of late. It's much more dangerous now. Life was terrible under the Russians, but now the Germans are making it impossible."

"Yes, Father John, I know. That's why I'm asking for your help. Won't you do it for my mother?" Laibale's voice quaked. "We've lost practically everything already. We might have to run for our lives one day, and I don't have anything but my motorcycle. I know that Peter has kept his word. He said he would keep my bike in good shape, for when I needed it."

"Let me think on it, my boy," the priest said, stroking his chin as he did when pondering something. "If I should agree, it would have to be done in secret. Maybe I wouldn't even know where Peter left it, just in case. Now we need to get back inside. I'm sure Nese has other parcels to deliver. We'll talk again later."

Laibale was relieved, encouraged that Father John hadn't refused his request outright. He felt almost happy.

He felt even happier when his mother told him their next stop was a special one. Laibale didn't realize they were headed to the Weinstein house until his mother whispered it to him as they walked down Father John's path. She had just finished some dresses for Mrs. Weinstein, including one that Rebekkah was planning to wear for a piano recital on Sunday.

When Laibale heard that he might see Rebekkah, his heart raced with expectation. Had his mother told him earlier, he might not have taken the time to speak with Father John. Still, Laibale was glad he had mustered the nerve to ask him. Somehow, Laibale believed Father John would help them. Even though the sewing basket wasn't heavy, Laibale took it out of his mother's hands and urged her to walk faster, excited at the possibility of seeing Rebekkah.

They arrived at the Weinstein's house just at dusk. When Rebekkah answered the door, Laibale could tell she was surprised to see him standing there with his mother. Laibale's mother spoke first. "Hello, Rebekkah," she said quietly. "I'd like to see your mother."

"Yes, of course, Mrs. Gillman. I'll get her."

Mrs. Weinstein invited them inside. But, Laibale decided to wait on the steps, as he wasn't entirely sure what he could possibly say to Rebekkah in front of the two mothers. It would have been so awkward. Just when he was regretting not having the nerve to go inside, Rebekkah opened the door and slipped quietly out to stand beside him. By now, it was fully dark, but Laibale could see her eyes reflected in the lamplight through the window. She was even more beautiful up close. Laibale felt his face grow warm. He was glad the darkness hid his blushing from her.

Rebekkah said, "Laibale, I hope you don't mind that I came outside."

Laibale took a deep breath and said, "I'm really glad you did. I've wanted to talk with you for a long time, but I guess I just haven't had the nerve."

"I feel the same way about you, too," Rebekkah said, much to Laibale's amazement. His heart lifted.

"You do? Well, how is it that you have never really spoken to me?"

"It seems that you never are alone much, that Joel is always around, and I just don't trust Joel. He has played so many tricks on my girlfriends."

"I know. Joel is hard to understand, but he's been a friend all my life."

"I don't guess we'll ever have the chance to become friends now," she said.

"What do you mean? Can't we just keep on talking until we get to know each other?" Laibale asked. He reached for her hand, hoping she wouldn't mind.

She stepped closer to him. She reached for his other hand,

causing Laibale's heart to thump so wildly he was afraid she could hear it.

"Oh, Laibale, I'm leaving tomorrow," she said, stifling a little cry. "Mother sent for the clothes early because she is sending me away. I won't even be here for the recital after all that practice."

Laibale's heart fell. "But I don't understand. Where will you go?"

"I have an uncle in America, in New York. Mother and Father are going to try to sell the business, but they want me out now. I leave on the first train to Germany in the morning. Mother has friends who will be taking care of me. From there, I'll board a ship to the United States."

Laibale suddenly felt like crying himself. Instead, he put his arms around Rebekkah, hoping she wouldn't pull back. Surprising him again, she rested her head on his chest and returned the hug.

Laibale's mouth went dry suddenly and his heart sped up even more. He leaned back a bit and asked, "Will I ever see you again?" When she didn't answer, he finally managed to ask, "How can I contact you?"

"My uncle is the president of the First National Bank in New York City," she whispered. "It's located on Fifth Avenue. You can write to me there. His last name is Weinstein as well. He'll get your letters to me."

The door opened, and Rebekkah stepped back so suddenly Laibale almost fell off the porch. The two mothers exchanged a knowing glance. Laibale's mother walked between him and Rebekkah down the stairs, followed by Mrs. Weinstein.

Mrs. Weinstein spoke first, her voice wavering slightly. "Thank you, Mrs. Gillman, for all that you've done for my family over the years." She hugged her a long time.

"Laibale, you take good care of her now, won't you?" Mrs. Weinstein put her hand on Laibale's elbow.

"I'll do my best, Mrs. Weinstein," Laibale answered, trying to sound brave.

"Come inside, Rebekkah," said Mrs. Weinstein. "We must finish your packing now that we have your dresses."

Rebekkah looked at Laibale, almost afraid. Suddenly she moved forward and gave him a quick hug and a kiss on the cheek, then turned and ran up the steps without looking back. Her mother smiled as she closed the door behind them. Laibale felt like a horse had kicked him in stomach. He swallowed hard. His mother started walking away quickly. Laibale took some deep breaths, picked up his mother's empty basket, and caught up with her. In silence, they walked toward home.

When they entered the square, they saw a huge group of people gathered around the public announcement area. Several men were holding torchlights. Some of them were even shoving each other aside to get a better look. As Laibale and his mother approached, Dr. Elkes, a very tall and respected medical doctor, began to read the announcement. Laibale stood quietly beside his mother and heard the terrible words that would end any free life for Jews in that area.

"The decree, from the mayor of Lithuania, demands that all Jews in this area move inside Slobodka. It will then be called Kovno Ghetto. We have three weeks to move in. All Jews outside the ghetto after August 15, 1941, will be executed."

Laibale and his mother walked home in stunned silence. Laibale's only comfort was that at least Rebekkah would make it out alive.

7

Leaving Home

Laibale eased open the screen door, trying not to wake his mother as he went out into the early morning. He scraped his elbow on a piece of dangling mesh wire poking out of one corner of the doorframe. As he reached to blot the blood on his arm, he suddenly felt guilty over not repairing the door. His mother had mentioned it several times, but he had been waiting for warm weather to do it. It was already mid-July, and she had reminded him more than once recently, but he had just kept finding reasons to put it off. Repairing it now would be futile. He certainly wasn't going to fix it now that they would be moving into the ghetto.

It was all he could do to keep from ripping the wire completely from the frame in frustration. Instead, he curled the frayed edges onto themselves to keep them from cutting anyone else, pushed open the door, and held it to keep it from slamming shut. He glanced out at the gray dawn and then shook his head to clear it. His thoughts kept running into each other, creating a muddle in his mind. He couldn't quite take in how suddenly their lives had changed.

He stepped outside and nodded to Mr. Brodecki and Mr. Zimm as they quietly opened their front doors, too. They always came out at daybreak to stretch their legs and smoke their first cigarette of the day. Today they didn't seem to notice Laibale. A rooster's crow broke the silence.

Laibale was surprised to see Joel approaching. He stepped close to Laibale, his face falsely serious. "It's a good morning for moving, don't you think?" Joel said in a phony, high-pitched voice.

"Yeah, mighty fine day," Laibale said and frowned. "Stop with the jokes, Joel. I found Mama crying in her bedroom again yesterday. All she's been talking about lately is leaving. Everybody's upset." He pointed at his neighbors. "I waved to Mr. Zimm and Mr. Brodecki just now, but looks like they didn't see me. They're having one serious conversation. Everybody's talking about what a hard time we're facing."

The sound of loud footsteps made him look down the street. A neighbor, Mrs. Goldstein, was running toward them.

"Laibale, Joel, come quick!" Mrs. Goldstein gasped as she reached them. "It's my husband!" She spun on her heel and starting running back toward her house a few blocks away, assuming they would follow. A fat woman who usually never walked above a slow saunter, she was running like wolves were chasing her.

Laibale and Joel caught up with her as she ran down the street.

"What's wrong?" Laibale shouted to her.

Slowing a bit, she wheezed, "He can't breathe! He was packing and just fell over!" Mrs. Goldstein ran again as they all turned down Paneriu Street. They saw Mr. Goldstein on his knees just in front of the house surrounded by boxes. One large box was split open, its contents askew, as if Mr. Goldstein had fallen on it.

Laibale knelt beside the wild-eyed man.

"Everything is going to be okay, Mr. Goldstein," Laibale said in a quiet voice, hoping the sweating man couldn't tell how his heart was pounding. "Here, let me help you lie down." He situated him in a prone position. "That's right, Mr. Goldstein. Easy. Take some deep breaths. Just try to relax. Everything is going to be okay."

A crowd gathered. A man shouted, "Go get Dr. Elkes!"

"Joel, put those blankets under his feet," Laibale said in a quiet voice. "Find something to fan him with. Mrs. Goldstein, loosen his belt and see if you can unbutton his collar some more." He turned to the crowd. "Stand back. He needs air."

Mrs. Goldstein followed Laibale's instruction, then stood up and began praying out loud. She fanned her husband, then herself. Joel moved closer and put his arm around her, temporarily losing his balance as she leaned most of her weight against him. A few moments passed before Mr. Goldstein's breathing eased. Laibale was relieved to see the normal color returning to his face.

Mr. Goldstein reached out a hand to touch Laibale's elbow. "When did you become a doctor?" he asked. "I thought you were a mechanic." A slight grin formed on his glistening face.

"We had first aid classes, Mr. Goldstein," Laibale said blushing. "If we were still in school, I'd get credit for this."

"Well, I'll give you credit anyway," Mrs. Goldstein said. She wiped a tear with her apron, bent over, and tried to hug Laibale at the same time. "He's a stubborn one." She pointed at her husband. "Always trying to do too much. The Rosenbaums were coming later. Do you think he would wait? No! He has to do everything by himself. I keep telling him, 'Slow down. You're not as young as you used to be.' Do you think he listens? No!"

Joel tried to be reassuring. "You just rest, Mr. Goldstein." He turned to Mrs. Goldstein. "Don't worry," he said. "Laibale and I will help move your things."

"That's right," Laibale replied. "Let me run home and tell Mama. I'll tell your mother, too, Joel. Will she be up yet?"

"She was making coffee when I left," Joel said. "Tell her to save me some breakfast."

"Okay," Laibale said. "Mrs. Goldstein, see if you can get your husband to drink a little something. Maybe it will cool him off some. Is that okay with you, Mr. Goldstein?"

"If that's the doctor's orders, what can I do?" Mr. Goldstein said with a little shrug of his shoulders and a weak smile.

Laibale ran home to find his mother washing dishes.

"Why aren't you packing, Mama? We only have one more day to report to the ghetto."

"You're *meshuggah*," she said, looking up. "We have two days. The order said August 15. Today is August 13."

"No it isn't," Laibale said, hitting his head with open palms and walking away while trying to stay calm. Facing his mother again, he took a deep breath and tried to keep a measured tone. "I thought we went over this a few days ago. Here, look at the calendar." He took the calendar off the small nail on the wall and showed it to her. "Today is August 14."

"What?" His mother dropped a plate in the sink and broke it. "Now look what I've done, broken one of my mother's best dishes." She looked at Laibale. Her voice trembled. "How could that be? I'm not ready! Are you sure?" Her voice rose in panic.

"Very sure," Laibale said, his voice softening at his mother's distress. "But you're not the only one who has the days mixed up. There's so much confusion with everybody coming and going. Start packing now. Please hurry! I'll be back as soon as I can."

"Back from where?" his mother asked, raising her voice. "I need you to help me. Your *bubbe* will try, but she can't do much."

"The Goldsteins need me more right now. Mr. Goldstein worked himself into a terrible state trying to move things."

"*Oy vey!* He hasn't been out of the hospital that long. I thought the Rosenbaums were going to help them."

"Mr. Goldstein wouldn't wait," Laibale said. "Joel is still with them. We promised to help. It shouldn't take too long. They only have one old sled. I'll get some twine while I'm here. We'll still have to pull it to the ghetto. I'll be back as fast as I can." Laibale rummaged through several drawers, turning things upside down while looking for the twine. He finally found it in the bottom of the third drawer.

"It's ridiculous," his mother said. "Mr. Goldstein has a perfectly good car that would hold a lot of their belongings." The anger showed on her reddened face. "I don't like the thought of my son being used as a horse. We'll probably all have heart attacks before this is over. I guess the Nazis think we'll take less if we have to move everything by sled or in wagons."

She started picking up the shards from the broken plate and throwing them into the trashcan. Suddenly, her anger was replaced with dismay. "What will I do?" she asked, looking dazed. "I can't be ready so fast. I need to wash clothes. How can I decide what to take and what to leave behind?"

"Where is the list I copied for you?" Laibale asked. "I put it on the cupboard." He moved a stack of plates and found the piece of paper and began reading aloud. "Only bare necessities are cleared for ghetto inhabitants. One chair for each person, minimum amounts of dishes, pots and pans, a bed or bedroll per person, four changes of clothing and underwear, two pairs of shoes."

"What? That means I can't take my dishes for Passover," his mother exclaimed. "Surely I can take my sewing machine," she reasoned. "Is there anything there about restrictions on sewing machines?"

"They're not allowed," Laibale said matter-of-factly. "Maybe I can hide yours inside a bedroll, but that means we'll have to leave something else behind. Even then, we'd be taking a terrible risk."

"My sewing machine, left behind?" His mother's voice was nearing hysteria and tears formed in her eyes. "How will we eat if I can't work?"

"You won't have to worry about working if you don't start packing soon."

As they stood there, Joel's mother, Mrs. Simon, opened the door.

"Oh, Nese!" she wailed as she let herself in. "This is terrible."

Laibale's mother nodded sadly. She walked to the door and stood beside her friend. "Who would have thought there would be no more candles prayed over at *Shabbat*, no more meals eaten in these houses where so many babies have been born?" Babies are supposed to be a blessing from God. And, where is God now?" She sobbed into her hands.

The mothers embraced tenderly.

"This is hard on everyone, but we have no choice," Mrs. Simon said. "I'm finished packing. I came to see if you needed help. Where do you want me to start?"

"I don't know," Laibale's mother said, holding her head with both hands. "What did you pack?"

"As little as possible," Mrs. Simon said. Some of the staunchness had drained out of her. "It's going to be unbearable with thousands of us crowded together."

Laibale's mother paused for a minute and put her arm around her friend. "Just think, Irena, by nightfall tomorrow all the houses will be empty."

"They'll be empty all right," replied Mrs. Simon. "Along with everything else. Remember to leave your doors, even the closet doors, as well as all the dresser drawers, open." She spoke in a menacing voice, mocking the order. "They probably want them open so the looters can easily steal what they want after we're gone."

"How will we manage?" Laibale's mother asked. "No running water! No inside toilets!"

"We'll probably have to stop bathing. I've heard there are only four wells for everyone and that electricity will be available only a few hours each day."

"God help us!" Laibale's mother said. "I can't imagine what it's going to be like with all of us packed in like fish in a barrel."

"I've been thinking of that as well. There will be no privacy, with three and four families having to live in one of those tiny houses."

"Mama," Laibale interrupted. "You'd better get busy here or you won't have anything packed at all when I get back from helping the Goldsteins."

"Yes, you're right," his mother replied. She turned to her dreadful task.

"Thank you for the help," Laibale said to Joel's mother.

"You're more than welcome, Laibale," Mrs. Simon said touching Laibale gently on the shoulder. "We all need to help each other right now." Laibale gave her a half-hearted smile before he went out into the street to help the Goldsteins.

8

Entering Kovno Ghetto

L aibale and his mother joined the final throng that lined up to get into the ghetto by the allotted time. There was pushing and shoving, causing such confusion that sometimes only a few items were checked by the guards as the people passed through the entrance gate.

As they approached the guard, Laibale dropped a blanket, spilling utensils on the ground.

"You stupid Jew!" a guard shouted, pushing Laibale down to the ground on his knees. "Pick it up and move on! I ought to make you leave it where it is! Can't you see we've got work to do?"

"I'm sorry, sir, really sorry," Laibale said, just as planned, scrambling to retrieve the pots and pans, actually kicking some even farther away. Because of the diversion, his mother managed to pass through the inspection line with her disassembled sewing machine undetected in a big suitcase.

Later, they arrived at their assigned quarters. Sara, Moshe and Sheina's daughter, ran through the front door to meet her grandmother. Once inside, Laibale's mother looked to see that her mother, Israel, and his girlfriend, Lola, had also arrived. Satisfied that all eight were accounted for, Laibale's mother lowered her voice and told them how she managed to smuggle her sewing machine inside the ghetto." Then she turned to Laibale with a wide grin and added, "You have a good head on your shoulders."

"Yes, it's a lot like yours, I believe," Laibale returned the compliment with his own smile. "I'm going out to find Joel now. Maybe some of the old ones need help."

Laibale found his friend quickly and offered to help Joel pull a sled filled to overflowing with an elderly couple's belongings. They made promises to others as they passed by. Some people had no relatives to help them unpack and get settled.

"Did you hear what Mr. November did this morning?" Joel asked as they wrestled with the sled.

"No," said Laibale.

"Well, I heard he beat the tar out of Mr. Bernstein."

"What, those two old men fighting? I thought they were friends."

"They used to be friends," Joel said. "Now they're threatening to kill each other."

"Why?"

"Bernstein tried to move into a house that November had already claimed. Said Bernstein didn't have as many kids as he did and needed less space."

"Sounds like everybody's fighting," Laibale said. "Mrs. Rose got into a terrible argument yesterday with Mr. Brodecki's wife. I heard they almost came to blows at the well." He shook his head. "Mrs. Rose! Our nice teacher."

"What happened?" Joel asked.

"Mrs. Brodecki seemed to think that because she had a husband, she should go first," Laibale said. "She's been looking to pick a fight anyway, ever since we got here."

"Yeah," Joel said. "I feel sorry for her. It was terrible how she had to leave her mother's body outside their house."

"Just awful," Laibale agreed. "You'd think the Germans could have at least let them bury her."

"When have you ever heard of Nazis having sympathy?" Joel asked.

"There will be no sitting *shiva* for her either," Laibale added. "Folks said she just dropped dead when it came time to move into the ghetto. I guess it was just too much of a shock."

"Well, some of the old ones who made the move aren't doing much better," Joel said. "My mother went over to help out that ancient couple, the Baers, and she said they just sat in the corner of their son's house together and cried."

"They have reason to cry," Laibale said. "Mr. Baer always told me that he was saving the pennies I spent on candy in his store. He said it helped him, as they had only one son to take care of them. Now most of what they worked for has either been stolen or destroyed."

Laibale and Joel continued to help the ones who needed it the most while assisting their own mothers. Gradually, some semblance of order was found inside the ghetto walls. The fights, which had become less frequent, turned into an occasional shouting match as families settled in and tried to comfort themselves with just being together.

Everyone fell asleep on the floor the first night. The second day, while all of them stumbled around boxes and belongings, Nese came up with a plan, trying to ensure some modicum of privacy.

"Moshe," she began, "You and Sheina and Sara can sleep in the bedroom. *Bubbe* needs warmth, so she and Lola and I will sleep on the kitchen floor. Israel, that leaves the parlor floor for you and the Little Lion."

"I'm sure I'll be well protected then," Israel said with a hint of sarcasm.

"Israel snores worse than a train," Laibale stated.

"I don't know how much sleeping any of us will do," Laibale's mother said. "Let's just be glad we have a roof over our heads. There are families with twenty people shoved into some of these tiny houses." She paused for a moment, walked around the kitchen, and added, "The worst part will be no running water and those awful outhouses. The first thing we've got to do is clean this place. Laibale, you and Israel find some buckets and bring me some water. Moshe, go find some wood so we can heat the water on the stove. Girls, get some rags and pick a place to start cleaning. This place is so dirty that it could take all day."

Laibale's mother set about unpacking boxes and arranging her dishes inside the cupboards. Sometime that afternoon, after Laibale had gone to help an elderly couple, he found his mother standing on a chair. She was using thumbtacks to secure lace curtains strung on a piece of elastic.

"What are you doing?" Laibale asked. "You mean you wasted space bringing curtains?"

"Well, I couldn't bring my Passover dishes, so I thought we should have something to remind us that we are still human beings."

Three days after the ghetto closed, there was sudden excitement. A notice had been posted on the newly designated court building. It didn't look like a court building, especially since it was old and gray and needed paint, like all the buildings in that area, but it was probably the best of the lot. It was also situated right beside the main gate, so no one could say they didn't see the announcements.

Laibale elbowed his way through the crowd. He called out to a friend at the front, "What does it say, Alex? Read it out loud." Laibale grew quiet and gave a wide berth to the guard holding a gun, afraid of what new restriction might be placed on them.

Alex said in a loud voice: "Tomorrow there will be a need for some 500 men for a special work detail." His voice got even louder as he became excited about what he was reading. "Only the most educated Jews, doctors, lawyers, teachers, anyone holding a college degree, should apply for this work. Those chosen will perform archival duty at one of the outlying forts and will be paid accordingly. Interested and qualified men should report no later than 7 a.m. tomorrow. Bring your lunch."

Laibale walked away in disgust. "Only the educated need apply," he said under his breath. "Well, I'd like to see some of those educated men take apart a motorcycle and put it back together again."

Early the next morning, Laibale stood looking out the kitchen door, wishing he could go with the band of men that was forming. As it turned out, 537 men had been selected for the work detail. They were laughing and teasing each other, breaking some of the tension for the first time since the ghetto was sealed.

"I'll go crazy if I have to keep staying inside this little space," Laibale said in a quiet voice.

His mother heard him. "I know you hate to be cooped up, Laibale, but something tells me this is going to turn out badly." She shook her head slowly with a sigh. "I'm glad you're not old enough to go. For once, I'm glad you don't have more education than you do, or I know you'd be in the thick of them." She sighed again. "Come on, I'll fix you some breakfast."

"They're leaving," Laibale reported, his shoulders going slack. "Wait a minute. Who is that coming back?" He pushed his head out just beyond the door to call to a neighbor, Menachim Beinstock. "Hey, Menachim, did you forget something?"

"Yeah, I wanted to kiss my new bride goodbye one more time," Menachim said with a wide grin on his face.

His young bride stood on her tiptoes, received the kiss, and waved as Menachim ran to catch up with the rest of the group. The men walked quickly, anxious to be outside the confines for the first time since the ghetto formed.

After they left, the day passed quietly. Everyone was trying to adjust to their cramped quarters.

Later, Laibale's mother swept the floor again and again, trying to make some semblance of order where all of them would be staying. She set the table for the evening meal. "It's suppertime, Laibale," she finally said. "Come in the house and light the candles."

"I don't think anyone's come home yet," Laibale said. He looked out the window and watched the street. A lone dog wandered by, searching for food scraps.

Candles flickered in the houses, as families waited, going to the front doors from time to time. Laibale, too, was anxious for a report of what had been accomplished and how much money had been made.

Long after supper, after the dishes were put away, Laibale's mother said, "It's 11 p.m." She began to pace in front of the door. "I knew I was right. They've come to no good end."

"Aw, Mama, you're just being negative," Laibale said. "Why do you have to be so suspicious? They're just working overtime, that's all."

"No one is working this late, I tell you," she replied. "At least it's a warm night, so we can leave the front door open and we'll hear them when they come home."

Laibale stepped outside later. There was so little noise in the ghetto that he could hear the clocks striking midnight from other houses. It sounded like a death knell.

Three days later, after not one man had returned, Joel ran into the house without knocking.

"Laibale, there's terrible news! Old November heard one of those damned German officers laughing about how the bodies had jumped when they shot them."

"What?" Laibale asked. His heart froze.

"They shot them. All of them."

"Are you sure?"

"Yes, I'm sure. I'll be back later. I have to tell Mama." Laibale stood in disbelief as Joel ran away. It was like a nightmare. He dreaded telling his mother but he knew she would hear it sooner or later.

"Shot? They've all been shot?" his mother said, practically shouting.

"Yes, Mama, it seems to be true. At least that's what Joel said."

"Well, we can't always believe Joel, but this time I fear he's right." His mother's shoulders sagged as if under a great weight. After a moment she put her arms around Laibale. He returned the hug, comforted by her presence. "This is one time that I'm sorry to be right," she said quietly.

Word began spreading through the ghetto like wildfire, followed by the wailing of women who could not be consoled.

Joel and his mother appeared at the door again about an hour later.

Mrs. Simon pushed open the door, her face ashen.

"What's wrong? Tell me," Laibale's mother demanded. "There couldn't be any more bad news."

Laibale and Joel stepped to the back of the room, trying to give the two women some privacy.

"It's Menachim's wife," Mrs. Simon began. "When she heard what happened, she cut her wrists. She bled a great deal, but Dr. Elkes thinks she'll pull through."

Laibale's mother caught her breath. "That poor child. What are we going to do?"

"We're setting up a schedule for someone to be with her for the next few days," Mrs. Simon said. "I thought you'd want to come."

"Of course I will. Of course I will," she whispered, her voice breaking. "I'll come for a few hours in the evening, whenever you need me. Just let me know."

Laibale and Joel stood helpless as the women's resolve finally broke. The two mothers sobbed in each other's arms briefly but then pulled away, as if suddenly realizing that Laibale and Joel were watching.

Laibale's mother wiped her eyes with her apron. "Well, we can't just stand here and cry. We've got to work together. Let me know when it's my turn to be with her."

"Of course. Of course." Mrs. Simon straightened her dress and she and Joel left.

Watching her friend go down the street, Laibale's mother grew quiet. She went into the bedroom and stayed by herself for a long time. Later, when she came out, her face was red from crying.

"You know, Laibale," she said as she placed an arm around Laibale's shoulders, "You were spared for a reason." Laibale didn't reply. He just held his head in his hands, trying hard not to cry himself.

Finally his mother said goodnight and then he fell into bed, exhausted. Laibale watched the last candle until it burned out. He couldn't stop thinking about how those men, some of them his longtime friends, had been so jubilant to be leaving the ghetto, looking forward to a day of work, of feeling like men again.

It was a long time before Laibale shut his eyes. His last thought was wondering whether he and his *bubbe*, mother, and all the rest of them would get out of the ghetto alive.

9

Unexpected Trouble

Months spent inside the ghetto hung around Laibale's neck like boulders, each one dragging him down more than the last. Surviving for a day was reduced to surviving for the next hour. One morning, Laibale heard his mother shriek.

"What's wrong? "

"It's your *bubbe*. I can't wake her up."

Laibale leaned over his grandmother's still body. He picked up her hand and held it gently, as he turned to his mother and quietly said, "We've lost her, Mama."

"My sweet Mama," Laibale's mother said, brushing tears from her eyes. "I so hate that she died here instead of in her own home."

Like Laibale's *bubbe*, other things began to wear out. Even with his mother's extraordinary sewing skills, their meager clothing became threadbare, hanging on their thinning bodies and making them look like walking shadows.

"You're beginning to look like a scarecrow," Laibale's

mother said one day.

"Well, I wish I was working in a garden instead of for the Nazis," Laibale replied.

"Maybe I can piece some things together and make you a better coat," Laibale's mother said, walking around him and looking at the frayed elbows of his jacket.

"You might not find anything to make it with," Laibale said. "Coats are in such demand now that dead people aren't even respected anymore."

"What are you talking about?" Laibale's mother asked.

"I saw something yesterday that I didn't think I'd ever see. Joel and I were walking through the streets and we saw some men taking coats off of dead men."

Laibale's mother shivered, as she remembered how the Russians had deported thousands of citizens to Siberia when they were in charge. Now the Germans were enforcing ever-worsening and even more unimaginable restrictions on the Jews.

"Have we become no more than animals?"

"Call it what you like, Mama, but people are freezing. Those men had to work fast, before the bodies got stiff."

"I can't believe that someone would be so disrespectful," Laibale's mother added.

"That's not all," Laibale said. "They were stripping off the boots as well. That part was pretty easy, though. It only took them a few seconds to strip the whole body completely. Then they ran away before the men's family found them."

"Oh, my God," Laibale's mother said in despair. Her face hardened with resolve. "I guess, though, that if that's what it takes to survive, we would do it, too."

To make matters worse, rations were severely reduced. Originally, a decent amount of food and even some firewood had been provided, but that was all short-lived. As winter truly set in, the drudgery got worse.

"The days are getting longer now. It won't be long before spring," Laibale said one day, as he brought in some broken boards he had managed to rip off a fence so his mother could cook their dinner.

"I know, I know," Laibale's mother replied, "but right now we have snow, and it hurts my bones and makes me irritable."

"Yeah, I noticed that you've been awfully cranky lately," Laibale teased. "Does that mean you will cook me some *lochen kugel* to make up for it?"

"Oh, Laibale, I wish I could cook something good for you," Laibale's mother said, her voice trailing off as she looked out the window.

"I know you would, Mama," Laibale said softly, stepping closer to his mother and wrapping an arm around her thin shoulders. "I just had to tease you a little. It's been a long time since I heard you laugh."

"Yes, it's very difficult now and not much to laugh about." Laibale's mother said. "Joel's mother even told me yesterday how Mr. Brodecki, that sweet pious old man, has barely been able to remain civil to his own family. Why, he used to be the temple leader. When the old ones who have been our leaders over the years stay angry all the time it makes me wonder how the rest of us will make it."

"We'll make it, Mama. You'll see," Laibale said with renewed confidence. "We'll make it because we'll all stick together and help each other."

"I hope you're right, Little Lion," Laibale's mother said with a smile as she touched his arm. "Now wash up and I'll see if I can't find some leftover *challah* bread and honey for you."

"Well, now, that's not exactly *lochen kugel,* but it sounds like a fine substitute until you can do better," Laibale said, enjoying the smile on his mother's face.

Everyone in the ghetto struggled to survive under the limited rations. A few people managed to grow and store vegetables in a communal gardening spot, which helped stave off starvation for some, but even those supplies were thinned by theft. It became necessary to post a guard at the garden sites and by the storage bins. The firewood eventually was gone, too. While some people resorted to stealing furniture and burning it while their neighbors were on work brigades, others stripped off parts of their own homes to use as fuel. Electricity was available for about four hours a day, but never in a consistent pattern. Sometimes the current was turned on while they were out on work details, forcing them to resort to kerosene lamps and candles at night.

One night, following a ghetto purging, Laibale rushed into the house to see if his family had been spared.

"Mama, I'm so glad to see you," he said, almost knocking his mother over with a hug.

"We were lucky this time," Laibale's mother said. "It seems that every time a new commander comes to the ghetto, he decides that there are too many Jews to feed and orders a selection. This time they were culling out families of ten. Lucky for us, there are only seven here."

Selections, the systematic gathering of certain groups, were carried out without prior notice. The ruse, that workers were needed in other camps, could not have been true, since the elderly and the young were the primary targets chosen for transport in the huge, canvas-covered trucks.

Illness took its toll as well. Although ghetto doctors tried valiantly to save lives, some prisoners simply lay down and died, their only respite from a meaningless existence. A never-ending stream of carts, pulled by men, picked up the bodies left beside the houses by family members. Sometimes the corpses remained for days, stacked like piles of wood alongside the outbuildings, frozen into stiff piles with icicles hanging from them, waiting for their transfer and burial at one of the fort sites in a huge grave.

But multiple deaths still did not seem to relieve the crowded ghetto. Like caged rats, some 35,000 Jews were crammed into a tiny space that was originally home to a few thousand individuals.

Laibale and Moshe were talking about the crowded conditions as they walked home from work one day.

"I've been thinking about moving," Moshe said. "Even with *bubbe* gone, we're still so crowded."

"Moving? Out of the ghetto?" Laibale asked in mock surprise.

"Of course not," Moshe said. "You know as well as I do that we can't move outside the ghetto. Maybe we can find a bigger house."

Laibale looked around at the tiny houses, many with broken windows, dilapidated and in need of paint.

"The only way to get an empty house is for people to be shot," Laibale said.

"Well, I'm not anxious to die," Moshe replied, "but death would at least be an escape from the ghetto."

"Don't even be joking about that, Moshe. We're all going to make it out alive," Laibale said, trying to convince himself along with his brother. "We just need to try and stay healthy, that's all. At least we're young."

"That's true," Moshe said. "I really worry about Mama, though."

"Well, we'll just have to do the best we can," Laibale said as they approached their house.

Rumors flew about the ghettos in surrounding areas being infested with typhus and other dreadful diseases. The doctors in Kovno Ghetto, trying to forestall a disaster, insisted on fastidious attention to cleanliness, especially inside the hospital. The Nazis also added their form of disease control.

Hospitalization for a few days was allowed, but staying longer than that resulted in a patient being shot.

Although despised, the hideous work details kept others alive. Everyone learned that, even when the body is starved, it functions better with routine. Before dawn every morning the Germans barked orders while the *kapos*, or Jewish guards who assisted the Germans, ran through the houses screaming at the inhabitants to get up and report for the count. Sometimes the workers had to stand for hours in the freezing rain and the snow. Anyone who fell was shot where they lay and dragged out of the lineup. Another person would be forced to fill the gap.

Laibale and Israel were standing at attention one day, waiting for the hated count to be finished. A man two feet away fell to the ground. No one reached to help him stand. Seeing the fallen man, a soldier ran down the line screaming, "Get up! "Get up, or I'll shoot you!" When the man didn't even raise his hand, the soldier drew his pistol and shot him in the head. Laibale and Israel didn't look but stared straight ahead, having grown numb to the insanity.

The daily assignments and the monotony of the work brigades changed little as the seasons came and went for the next two years. The morning routine never deviated. Prisoners had to stand five abreast, hands by their sides, looking straight ahead. Sometimes they stood for interminable hours waiting for the *kapos* to verify the desired number of workers. The guard would finally call out, "Forward."

With the approved order, the workers began marching through the main gate of the ghetto, passing another *kapo* posted at the entrance. His leather boots, knee-length wool coat, hat, scarf, and gloves made the workers want to kill him. The Star of David on his armband was probably the only thing that saved him during the long nights.

One day, as Laibale's line approached the gate, he was

directed to wait. He craned his neck to watch his mother's brigade until they turned to the left and passed out of the gate. Although his mother was delicate and just barely five feet tall, she worked with nine other women in a coal-shoveling brigade, filling up boxcars for twelve hours a day. The night before, Laibale had watched her peel a few scrawny potatoes. He couldn't help but notice how the hands that once stitched such fine needlework were now twisted and hard with calluses. But, she never complained.

Screams interrupted Laibale's thoughts.

"You filthy Jew," one of the Nazis shouted to a worker. "Are you trying to sabotage the Reich? Get back to your brigade if you want to live." The Nazis continued beating the head of the poor fellow who had been attempting to avoid airport duty, the most hated assignment of all.

Moshe and Israel had been assigned to the duty early on several occasions because they were strong men. Sometimes Laibale was sent there, too. But most of the time he was directed to a garage where his mechanical expertise came in handy for repairing the jeeps or motorcycles for the Nazis, an assignment that sometimes caused resentment among the other men.

"We should all know how to use wrenches," Israel had said in a nasty tone just a few days earlier. He had returned from the airport that night with both hands bleeding, the result of blisters being worn away from shoveling all day.

Always the peacemaker, Moshe quietly said, "Leave Laibale alone. You know he means more to us here than outside the ghetto. At least he can fix the radios when they break down, and neither of us can do that."

"What good is news of the Russian army?" Israel hissed in a low voice. "By the time they get here, we'll all be dead from starvation or frostbite."

"Quit complaining," Moshe said, raising his voice uncharacteristically. "You're just jealous because Laibale gets to work where there's some heat." His voice softened a bit and he added, "Come on," he added. "Let me help bandage your hands."

More often than not, the two older brothers had to work at the airport every day. It was a treacherous assignment, standing shoulder-deep in trenches dug to drain off the daily rain that pooled on the runway. The work was vital to the German war effort, as the closest landing strip was about 30 miles away. Israel and Moshe usually got into the trenches, standing with their backs to each other. They had learned, through trial and error, that they could work better together than any of the other men. They shoveled the gravel that had run off with the rain over their backs to several men standing at the edge of the trenches. Those men, in turn, carried it in shovels back to the runway. All of them stood ankle-deep in mud working to keep the runway flat for the German planes, an exercise that was also thinning the ghetto ranks daily.

The worst part, Moshe always said, was the running. While the German guards rode bicycles along the way screaming for the prisoners to move faster, the men were forced to run about three miles to the worksite. Those who were too weak or hobbled from sore feet were simply shot and left on the road. The only reward for the effort was a cup of hot watery brown liquid that was supposed to be coffee, the Germans' excuse for breakfast.

When night began to close in, those left in the ghetto watched the gate for the returning work brigades. Just because a person went to work didn't guarantee that he would return. Often, especially if there was a cruel guard, prisoners were shot simply for the sport of it.

The repeated routine of inspections and counting changed only when new guards were assigned, each usually more sinister than the last. The routine seemed comforting, though, as it would take months for the tension of the latest selection to pass off. Every day that the brigades formed meant that there probably would be no selection in which hundreds would be summarily singled out and killed at the nearby forts.

Laibale had managed to convince the Germans that Joel was needed as his helper in the garage. Laibale maintained that Joel would help him work faster. The Germans agreed to his request, since Laibale had proved his mechanical ability on more than one occasion. One night, when Laibale and Joel had finished their work, they closed the garage door and were watching the brigades return as a truck pulled up to the garage, loaded with motorcycles and new parts.

"Well, Laibale, my friend," Joel said, "unless we get shot, it looks like we'll both be busy for quite a while. I guess that's what you call job security, right?"

Laibale clapped Joel on the back, thankful for a little joke in the midst of misery.

A German officer jumped out of the truck. "Where are you going?" he demanded.

"We've finished for the day," Joel said.

"You'll be finished when I say you're finished," the German spat. "I want one of these bikes fixed in the next hour, and I'm staying to see that you do it."

Joel slowly reopened the garage doors, and Laibale set the toolbox on the workbench again. He started retrieving the tools, preparing to inspect the bike. Joel walked up beside him and leaned over the bench.

"Say that we can't fix it, Laibale," he muttered. "I'm starving. Make this lousy Kraut wait another night for his ride."

Suddenly the German was standing beside them with his gun drawn. He pulled the trigger so fast Laibale didn't have time to react.

Joel's body slumped forward, blood spurting from his chest onto Laibale as he gathered him into his arms. Joel's head wobbled like an apple on a tree branch.

"Get him out of here," the German said. "I'll need that bike in an hour."

Laibale managed to drag Joel's limp body just outside the shed before he started vomiting. He ran back inside, his hands trembling as he tried to wipe Joel's blood off his hands and find the proper tools. He had to concentrate hard to repair the bike, which took him about half an hour. As the guard rode away, Laibale despised his talent for the very first time in his life. He looked down at his hands, sick at heart, realizing that he had aided his best friend's murderer.

Laibale sat beside Joel's body for a long time, too numb to cry. Only then did he think to say *Kaddish*, the prayer for the dead. He took off his thin jacket and spread it across Joel's chest, not wanting to see his friend's blood. It got so cold that he began to shiver. He rose slowly, his fingers numb. Joel's body was too big for him to take home alone. Laibale didn't even remember walking home until he saw the lamplight through the window. He didn't know how he was going to tell Joel's mother that her only child was dead.

10

Resistance

Several months later, Laibale's mother yelled for him to get up.

"Hurry, Laibale. Get dressed. I can hear them coming."

Outside, German soldiers shouted orders for them to line up and be counted. The door slammed as his mother ran out to take her place. Since Laibale slept in his shirt and socks, all he had to do was shove his legs inside his pants and grab his shoes. Soon he was outside, too. The chill in the air cut through his thin clothes. Even his mother's patching skill wasn't enough to keep him warm. The vines had died in the garden plots long ago, and each morning there was either frost or snow on the ground. Laibale rubbed his hands together and shivered in the cold.

Several guards fired their weapons into the air. They screamed, "*Schnell! Schnell!* Fast! Fast!"

As they struggled to line up, Laibale remembered something his mother had whispered into his ear after everyone had gone to bed.

"Laibale, I'll be bringing in a package tomorrow night. You must try to divert the guard during the count when I return."

"It's too dangerous, Mama. You'll be shot if they catch you. No food is worth your life. Please don't do it." Laibale was begging.

"You worry too much, Laibale. Where do you think you got that courage of yours?" She laughed nervously. "I know these guards well. I've always managed to bribe the one who will be on duty tomorrow. He loves eggs."

Laibale worried anyway. On rare occasions, prisoners dared to slip away from work details to either steal food or barter for it. Sometimes it cost them their lives, but they rationalized their efforts, knowing they were dying anyway. The ghetto rations, barely enough to sustain life, had been cut yet again earlier in the week, making the search for food all the more desperate. A few guards, the ones with an ounce of humanity left, sometimes walked away from their posts, offering a rare opportunity for the prisoners to trade the few baubles they had left for food from the villagers passing by the barbed wire fence that surrounded the ghetto.

While Laibale's mother was right about some of the guards taking bribes, Laibale had also seen them turn on returning workers, confiscating their treasures during an inspection at the gates. Retribution was swift when that happened, especially if a ranking German was on hand. The booty was confiscated, and the offender was either shot outright or sent immediately to either Fort VII or Fort IX, never to be seen again. All of them lived in dread of being taken to one of the forts. Those forts, hideous dark places on the outskirts of Kaunas, had originally been built by the Russians for fortification against encroaching armies. Since the ghetto's formation, the Germans had used them for executions.

Even with that threat, Laibale's mother took the risk and managed to bring in some form of food on a regular basis.

Sometimes it was only a few potato peelings, but she was good at getting past the guards. Even though she was very thin and practically dressed in rags, she had a regal manner about her that caused her to stand out among the other disheveled women in the ghetto. And, because she was so pretty, the guards allowed her some leeway, although she never favored them or gave them a reason to treat her differently. Always interested in languages, she spoke passable German, which probably endeared the guards to her even more. They considered anyone who didn't speak German a buffoon.

Laibale grew even more nervous when a new guard was unexpectedly assigned to the ghetto entrance a few hours ahead of schedule. Laibale had seen him through a garage window as he entered the ghetto earlier in the day. Actually, he had heard him before he saw him. The guard must have had stomach trouble, as he belched loudly as he walked by, adding to his already sour disposition.

Laibale stationed himself near the guard gate to wait for his mother's return. Within minutes, a little boy ran up to him and pulled on his jacket.

"Laibale, your brother wants you to come home as quick as you can," he whispered and ran off before Laibale could ask him anything.

When Laibale entered the house, Moshe shouted, "Laibale, Laibale, they've arrested Mama!"

"Where is she?"

"I don't know. I just got here myself."

Moshe and Laibale ran to meet Israel's work brigade, which had just arrived. When Moshe recounted what he had heard, that their mother had been caught with two eggs, Israel fell to his knees and rocked back and forth as he wept.

"Why did she do it? Why did she do it?" he moaned over and over.

"You know very well why she did it," Moshe said, pushing his older brother back with his hand. "Aren't you the one who kept complaining about being so hungry, about needing food for your girlfriend?"

"Stop it, both of you!" Laibale shouted. "Now is not the time to fight."

The three of them walked back toward home in silence, each lost in his thoughts about their mother and what she must be enduring. Just as they approached the house, Benjamin Green, a young man who had befriended Laibale in the ghetto, ran up to them and confirmed their worst fears.

"They've taken your mother to Fort IX," Benjamin managed to say, trying to catch his breath. "They got my brother, too, the bastards. I've got to tell my mother." He left as quickly as he had arrived.

The three brothers entered the house and stood in stunned silence, their hands in their pockets, unable to think of a way to resolve the dilemma. Israel's girlfriend, Lola, started peeling the few scrawny potatoes they had. Sheina struggled with how to tell Sara that her grandmother wouldn't be coming home that night. Their meager rations proved to be more than enough food for a change, as none of them were hungry. Instead, they all kept to themselves and went to bed early. Laibale couldn't sleep, but listened to the clock strike hour after hour, trying to think of how he might save his mother.

When the Germans started shouting for lineup the next day, Laibale remained in bed.

"Get up, Laibale," Moshe said. "Get up. They'll shoot you."

"Then let them," Laibale said and turned his back to his brother. Within a few minutes, a Nazi soldier kicked him in the back with his boot.

"Why aren't you at the count, you filthy Jew? You know we have motorcycles that need repair."

"Then do it yourself," Laibale said, without even turning over.

"You dare to talk to me in such a way?" The German dragged him onto the floor by his shirt collar and kicked him in the face. "Stand up."

Laibale stood and wiped the blood dripping down his chin, but didn't move toward the door.

"Get out!" the guard shouted, shoving Laibale. "Get out! We must have the count!" The guard was tall; he loomed over Laibale.

Laibale looked straight ahead and stood his ground. "I'm not going anywhere. How can I think of repairing motorcycles when you have my mother locked up in Fort IX?"

The Nazi's neck and face turned so red Laibale thought he was going to explode. Instead, he grabbed Laibale by the collar and pushed him out the door, where he forced him onto a motorcycle. The guard mounted the motorcycle in front and told Laibale to hold on. Laibale had never been so close to a Nazi before, much less put his arms around one. When the soldier gunned the motorcycle, though, Laibale had no choice but to grab him around the waist. Within minutes, the guard stopped and went inside a shed, returned with a gun, got back on the motorcycle, and headed down Paneriu Street toward Fort IX. Laibale was sure his fate was sealed and that he was riding to his death. Well, he thought, at least he would be with his mother.

But it turned out differently.

Later that night, Israel laughed as he remembered the scene.

"Oh, Laibale! When you rode out with that German, we thought you'd be executed, along with Mama. None of us could believe our eyes when we saw all of you coming back. Mama was sitting on the handlebars, hanging on for dear life. And, you were hanging on behind the German and he was trying to hang on to his gun. I tell you, that was something to see. No Jew has ever been taken *out* of Fort IX by gunpoint."

Israel laughed so hard he cried. Laying his hand on Moshe's shoulder, he said, "Brother, I have to admit you're right. The Little Lion is definitely worth more to us inside the ghetto."

11

Demokratu Square

There had been no major selections carried out for a long time, which made Laibale and everyone else very uneasy. They knew, from past history, that it could not go on forever. So they were not surprised when a notice was posted for a major assembly, one that would affect every prisoner in Kovno Ghetto.

Lines began forming long before dawn the next morning. Laibale stood with the door open and tried to keep count, but too many people were streaming by the house. He didn't know so many Jews still lived in the ghetto. In fact, he didn't know so many Jews lived in all of Lithuania. As far as Laibale could see, there were thousands of bowed heads, bodies leaning forward, a human herd moving almost in lock step before him.

Laibale watched as people, hundreds abreast, jostled for their places, huddling together trying to stay warm in the gray fog and drizzling rain, some of them pushing and rushing to be first in line. A few of the mothers tore off bits of bread from loaves they had brought along and periodically stuffed them into their children's mouths to keep them quiet. There had been no time to prepare hot food. Some of the older children carried the younger ones on their backs.

Laibale had read the order that had been posted on the public square the day before. Everyone living in Kovno Ghetto, every single person, had to be in Demokratu Square before the sun came up the next day. Even the hospital had to be emptied. A few of the nurses who had tried to protect the many orphans created by earlier selections now urged them to hold hands and form a line. Even so, some of the little ones became unattached and just stood at the edge of the crowd crying or looking bewildered, trying to find a familiar face. The order was clear. Anyone not reporting to Demokratu Square would be executed.

As the crowd moved forward, the sporadic sound of gunfire and screams from the hospital punctuated the air, signaling the fate of the women who had just given birth, their babies, and those too sick to walk out of the surgical wards.

The elderly ones in the moving mass were the worst. Some of them hobbled along, their feet somewhat protected by strips of old tires they had managed to salvage and tie onto their feet with bits of twine. Others, with no shoes, left patterns of blood, which were then stamped out or enlarged by fresh blood deposited by those who followed. Laibale watched as an old man fell to the ground just a few feet from where he was standing. He seemed to be pulling away from a young man who was trying to assist him. Looking closer, Laibale recognized a former school buddy and his grandfather.

"*Zeyde*," the young man pleaded to the old man. "You must walk. Come, I will help you." He slipped his hands under his grandfather's armpits to lift him up.

But his grandfather protested. "I cannot. Leave me. It is better I should die here."

"We're not going to die," his grandson said, dropping to his knees. He put his arms around the old man's shoulders and attempted to lift again but only managed to turn him toward the right. "You see," he said. "Look ahead. Everyone is lining up. They are just counting us again, so we can be divided into work brigades. It's just a count. Just like yesterday. No one will die."

"This time is different," the old man answered. "I can feel it inside." He touched his fingertips to his heart. Looking as if he might stand again, he managed to pull free. He sat upright long enough to straighten his long black coat. He looked into grandson's face, reached his hand up to touch his cheek, and then in a swift movement stretched out face forward on the ground, covering the back of his head with his hands. He lay so still that Laibale thought he had had a heart attack and had stopped breathing. He never looked up again, although his grandson kept pleading with him and trying to turn him over. No amount of coaxing would move him.

A line of people had begun forming on either side of them when a tall man said, "Get out of the way." He deliberately stepped into the center of the old man's back.

"Stop! Stop!" the grandson screamed, tears streaming down his face. "You can't walk on my *zeyde*." He began flailing his arms, attempting to stave off the growing swarm of people pressing forward. Soon realizing his efforts were futile, he sank to his knees again, began weeping out loud and rocking back and forth as the moving mass trod over the old silent man, his arms now outstretched. His fingers clawed the dirt and his beard became one with the earth.

As the crowd moved forward, Laibale saw another schoolmate, a girl he knew. When she saw the old man ground into the mud, she started vomiting. The crowd barely parted to give her breathing room, as everyone kept walking, the shuffling feet drowning out the grandson's bereft sobs as he continued his lamentation on his knees.

Laibale's mother was finally ready. She and Laibale waited for an opening and slipped out the door and into the throng along with Sheina, Moshe's wife. Sheina had a hard time keeping up, as she pushed a pram holding her daughter, Sara, who was not yet three years old. Sara had been asleep when Sheina gently placed her in the pram, but the jarring of the rutted street woke her. She let out a piercing wail.

"Keep that *tayvl* quiet," hissed a powerfully built, middle-aged Jewish man from just in front of them.

"She's hungry," Sheina offered in response. She tried to comfort Sara while she rearranged the thin blanket over her.

"And who's not hungry?" the man threw back, spitting out the words. "Better to be hungry than dead, don't you think?" He glared at her. He fell back a few feet, stepped toward Sheina and jabbed a finger into her chest. "If you can't keep her quiet, I'll do it for you." He made a move toward Sara, who shrank back in terror.

Sheina recovered enough to place herself between the man and the pram. She bent over, retrieved Sara, and practically threw her across her right shoulder.

The sudden movement frightened Sara even more, causing her to scream louder. Sheina wrapped the blanket tightly around her and shifted her to the opposite shoulder. Sara continued to wail and tried to escape her mother's arms, her cries now rising to a frenzied pitch.

Laibale knew he would be no match for the man, so he grabbed Sara, quickly loosened the blanket around her, placed her on his hip, and balanced her with his left arm. He handed the sack of food he was carrying to his mother and with his free arm, grabbed the pram and dragged it after him, putting some distance between him and the man who glared at them.

Sara grew quiet and sucked her thumb, now interested in the lines of strangers. She clung to Laibale's arm and looked over his shoulder. He fell into step, finally seeing some families he knew who used to live nearby.

"Who's the Nazi?" Laibale managed to ask the man walking just in front of him.

"That's Sergeant Helmut Rauca. They say he's taking over the ghetto."

"What are they doing?" Laibale asked. "Why are they separating one family from another?"

"Don't be a damn fool. You know very well there is a selection going on. One way means death, the other means we live a little while longer, but who knows which way is which?" The man shrugged his shoulders and turned away.

Laibale wondered where his brother Moshe was. Why couldn't he stay up with the rest of the family? It wasn't Laibale's place to take care of his brother's wife or his child. Suddenly Laibale felt ashamed as he remembered Moshe had risen very early to leave the house. Moshe had decided last night that he should help the Goldsteins. Mrs. Goldstein couldn't walk very fast and Moshe was probably steadying her so she wouldn't look so frail as they inched their way toward the German soldiers at the front.

Laibale thought of the old man buried in the mud, his life now just a memory. He shuddered and hugged Sara even tighter, as he, too, began to fall behind. He silently prayed that Sara would remain quiet as he returned her to the pram again and pushed his way through the crowd to try to rejoin his mother and Sheina. Laibale had to find them again, quickly. He was the only man they had to rely on.

The sun began breaking over the broad shoulders of Sergeant Rauca. Laibale guessed him to be more than six feet tall, but he looked much taller in his hateful uniform, like a giant standing with his feet wide apart glaring down at those who stood in front of him. One man from each family group stepped forward and identified himself as the spokesman to a soldier seated at a long table. There were stacks of papers on the table, some of them held down by rocks. Another German soldier scribbled notes on the paper directly in front of him. Every few minutes, Rauca leaned over and they had a discussion of some type, and then the soldier would rearrange the stacks of paper.

A man stepped up to stand by Laibale. It was Rabbi Creditor, the Gillmans' rabbi, who had always been special to Laibale. When Laibale had been preparing for his bar mitzvah a few years back, the rabbi had spent many hours helping him study and read from the Torah in Hebrew.

"Can you hear what they are saying?" Rabbi Creditor asked, keeping his voice low as he stepped very close to Laibale.

"Only that they are asking what we do for a living," Laibale answered.

"I shall be safe then," the rabbi said, as he stood straight with confidence. "Rabbis have always been respected in Lithuania."

Laibale hoped the rabbi was right. He was truly a man of God.

Another man stepped forward to face Rauca.

"What is your profession, damn Jew?" Rauca shouted, his voice now clearly audible.

The man trembled, fear choking his answer to a whisper.

"A cabinet maker," Rauca responded. "Get out of here then, you and your filthy urchins." Rauca sneered and pushed the man to the left toward the area where a small group of people had been congregating as they watched and waited for loved ones. The man quickly gathered his family and trotted in the direction Rauca was pointing, pulling a child by the hand as he went.

The soldier at the table offered Rauca a sandwich. Rauca slowly unwrapped it and tore the sandwich in half. He began eating out of the middle, not letting his lips even touch the crust, which he threw to the ground. He watched as two little boys dove for the bread and began to fight over it. Rauca kicked first one then the other, sending them sprawling. He then stepped on the bread, and ground it under his heel.

Rauca looked up to see the reaction of the crowd. The tension was so high that there seemed to be a shortage of air to breathe. Rauca touched the pistol on his side briefly and then motioned for the next man to step forward. No comfort was offered to the children who lay holding their sides and sobbing where they had been kicked.

Finished with his sandwich, Rauca picked up a cup of coffee with his right hand and began to sip from it. He held a riding crop in his left hand, which he flicked against his high-top polished boots. Every few seconds, after he studied the group in front of him, Rauca motioned either to the right or to the left with the crop, cutting the air with a whistling sound, as he sent groups to the right or left, methodically thinning the crowd.

Just as Rabbi Creditor was assuring his wife and children that all would be well, Laibale noticed Rauca's whip, pointing one of the Jewish doctors to the right with his family. He was ordered to join a huge group of people who were walking back toward Paneriu Street, the main road that ran in front of the ghetto toward the old Russian forts on the outskirts of town. Everyone in the ghetto knew the fate of those sent to the forts. When the doctor resisted joining them, two Nazi guards began beating him about the shoulders and head with batons and yelling at the crowd, "Move! Move! Faster! Faster!" Dr. Elchanan Elkes, the head of the Jewish Council, stood for hours beside Rauca, refusing all offers to sit, eat, or drink, pleading to save some of the families. At times, Rauca relented and let a few live.

Rabbi Creditor's family was next. Laibale could hear the rabbi, a proud man who always spoke with great confidence in the community, pleading for his family. He offered to be divided from them, anything for them to live. Rauca spat on him, then raised the whip and struck the rabbi in the face. To Laibale's amazement, Rabbi Creditor just stood taller and didn't flinch as Rauca sliced his crop through the air. With blood streaming down his face, Rabbi Creditor gathered his four children around him and tried to comfort his wife, who was now openly sobbing. They, too, were sent into the same direction as the doctor's family. Who could be more important than a doctor and a rabbi? Laibale wondered, as the rays from the morning sun broke through the clouds and bounced off the swastika insignia on Rauca's hat.

The sight of Rauca nauseated Laibale. But he swallowed hard. He couldn't be sick now. It was suddenly their turn. Laibale joined his mother and Sheina just as they reached the front of the line. Thankfully, Sara remained quiet, sucking her thumb even harder and watching the crowd from inside the pram as they edged closer and closer to the soldiers. Laibale wondered if any of them would live to see another sunrise.

12

The Family Lives

Laibale stepped up to Rauca. He felt something brush against him from behind. Turning his head slightly he saw Moshe out of the corner of his eye. Israel was there as well. As the oldest brother, Moshe was responsible for being the family spokesman. With a sigh of relief, Laibale started to move back, but Rauca poked him in the chest with his riding crop, demanding his attention.

Laibale used his hands to straighten his crumpled shirt, looked straight ahead, and practically shouted, "Good morning, Herr Rauca." He hoped to divert the officer's attention from his mother, who was leaning heavily on Moshe.

"Who are you to address me by name, you filthy swine?"

"Everyone knows who you are and respects your position here, sir," Laibale replied and stretched up to his full height of five feet and three inches.

"Look at the little dog with the big ears," Rauca said to the soldiers seated at the table. Rauca walked in a circle around Laibale, running the riding crop across his chest and over his shoulders. Laibale prayed that the man couldn't feel him trembling as he laid the crop across his right ear first and then over the left one. Rauca stopped in front of Laibale and shoved his face close to his.

"What he lacks in height he makes up for in ears," Rauca said. He broke out in a belly laugh as he looked toward the officer seated at the table.

"With those dog ears, you should hear all the news in the ghetto," Rauca added, rimming Laibale's right ear with the crop again. Finally, he spat on the ground, got even closer, and shouted, "What is your profession, damn Jew?"

Laibale's fear, mixed with Rauca's sour breath, made him nauseated. Raising his chin straight up, Laibale dared to look into Rauca's eyes for the first time. "I'm an excellent motorcycle mechanic, sir."

"Not just a motorcycle mechanic, Herr Malcolm," Rauca spoke up, both of them laughing now, "but an 'excellent' motorcycle mechanic."

Laibale took a breath. "Yes, sir. The Reich has excellent motorcycles, but they can always use good mechanics."

"And so it can, little dog," Rauca said. He paused for a minute, then quickly turned to the soldier keeping count, raised the crop, and said, "Let them pass."

Laibale watched as Sheina practically ran past the Germans, pushing the pram. She was followed close behind by Moshe, Israel and Lola, and Laibale's mother. Just beyond Rauca, Sheina grabbed Sara from the pram and covered her with kisses. Laibale staggered toward a shed. He barely made it out of sight before he fell on his knees and began heaving.

"There, there, Laibale," he heard his mother say. It seemed as if her voice came from far away. Only when she touched his head did he realize she actually stood beside him.

"What would we do without our Little Lion?" she asked softly. She wiped Laibale's mouth with a corner of her dress.

Laibale stood and embraced her. He felt her backbone through the big coat she wore. He couldn't help but think of the old man who had been trampled in front of them.

"Don't cry," she said, almost in a whisper, as Laibale wiped his nose on his coat sleeve and tried to regain his composure. "We've made it through another day."

Laibale's mother slipped her hand through his arm. Together they braced each other and started walking again. The empty houses they passed seemed to scream out in silence. Doors stood ajar. The returning prisoners darted in and out, carrying first clothes and then anything they could manage. Some dragged pieces of furniture belonging to their former neighbors. The Germans had already ransacked the houses, breaking much of what they had left. Very little that had any value remained. Still, it was an improvement over what some of them had. Larger families ran to make claims on the bigger houses, sometimes throwing out chairs to make room for beds. Many had been sleeping six to a bed or on the floor. At first, Laibale looked at them with disgust, then shrugged his shoulders. He could hardly blame them for trying to find a little comfort in this hellhole.

When they approached Rabbi Creditor's house, Laibale stopped and stood for a long time. He straightened an unpainted board that framed the front door. His mother stepped back a little and silently watched. Laibale then touched the family's *mezuzah*, which contained writing from the scriptures. He brought his fingers to his mouth, a sign of respect for the scriptures that commanded them to mount the words on their doorposts. But it was also a final tribute to Rabbi Creditor, who was surely facing imminent death.

The rabbi's rich baritone voice, when he was teaching Laibale to read the Torah, rang in his ears from memory. "I am the Lord your God. You shall have no other God before me...."

Laibale imagined the rabbi standing ramrod straight just now saying *Kaddish*, the prayer for the dead, as he walked with his family to their fate. As he stood by the empty home, Laibale wondered if he himself could ever be so brave.

Laibale's mother gently touched him on the shoulder, breaking his thoughts. He took her outstretched hand and finally moved on in silence.

Just then Moshe looked back. His face broke into a grin when he saw the rest of his family.

"Ah, Laibale," he called out. "Did you ever think you'd be glad to walk by those guards and be thankful to be inside these damned barbed wire fences again?" Moshe asked, laughing. Laibale couldn't help but grin at his brother.

"No, brother, I didn't," Laibale shouted ahead. It only lasted a second, but Moshe's laughter reminded Laibale that they were still alive, that their world of mud roads and limited electricity might now seem like a paradise to those sent in the other direction toward the forts.

"Laibale," his mother called out. Her voice was excited, as if her oldest son had suddenly wakened her from a bad dream. "Run quickly. Gather some firewood. Moshe, draw at least two buckets of water from the well. I have a few carrots and potatoes. If we hurry, I can cook them before sundown."

"I think I have part of a candle," Lola offered. The thought of prayers to bring in *Shabbat* invigorated them all. It was a time to be thankful. Realizing their good fortune, they hugged each other, moved quickly, and dared not to glance behind them for fear Rauca would change his mind and call them back.

After the women prayed over the tiny candle, Moshe, the oldest male, should have prayed over the bread. Instead, Israel made a quiet observation.

"I think the Little Lion should offer the prayer tonight. After all, he's the one who got us through the selection."

Bowing their heads in prayer, being together, and sharing the watery soup, their first meal of the day, relaxed them and pushed back the darkness of the day's events.

"Let's try to get some rest," his mother finally offered. "At least we have all made it another day."

The next morning a volley of gunfire woke Laibale. He covered his ears, wishing he couldn't hear so well. Repeated shots of the execution squads were the only sounds he could hear. Out of sight, he could only imagine the carnage that was taking place. The shooting continued for hours. Around midday, when silence finally came, an eerie calm fell over the house and the people in it, a gray silence like a fog that masked the life still within. No one dared to speak of the ones taken, as if words would crack the walls they had each carefully erected around themselves.

No one could even cry. They were all too shocked to comprehend it. Surely thousands of gunshots had been fired just that morning. How many had died? Usually just the old ones and young children were taken. But Laibale knew that entire families, and even entire generations, had been wiped out this day in a place called Demokratu Square.

Laibale, finally dared to break the silence. He whispered to his mother, "I've heard of democracy and even studied it some in school, but I never read that democracy and firing squads went hand in hand."

13

Quiet Prevails

Quiet fell upon the ghetto like a shroud. It seemed to permeate the houses themselves. Few people spoke above a whisper. Even though the children had previously known that silence was best, it was as if they somehow now understood in a deeper sense that a spoken word would draw attention to the people who were gone. They all lived in constant fear of being killed themselves, should their voices be heard.

Each person followed his own routine, knowing that their only reason for living was to serve their captors. Even the bravest ones had been cowed by the big selection, proving that no one was safe any longer, regardless of their profession. The last thinning seemed to be the final straw that broke the will of the ghetto, even though they were still secretly praying for the partisans, the resistance fighters living nearby in the forests. Word reached the ghetto one day that the partisans had commandeered some guns and had scored a victory by blowing up a bridge.

"Did you hear about what Chaim Yellen managed to do?" Laibale asked his brothers that night.

"No," Israel answered. "You know we've been at the airport all day. What happened?"

"Well, you know that Chaim escaped from the ghetto just three nights ago."

"Yes, I did hear that, but I didn't know if it was true or not," Israel said.

"It's true all right," Laibale said, enjoying how he could bring good news to share for a change. "I overheard two Nazis talking about how the bridge crumbled when it was dynamited."

"How did you get that kind of information?" Moshe wanted to know.

"I was working on their motorcycles. They thought they were far enough away from me not to hear, but these ears can hear a pin drop in the snow," Laibale said, laughing and pulling on his right earlobe before continuing. "They suspect Chaim was the chief orchestrator, especially since he was a demolition expert. Evidently, he reached the partisans just in time to help orchestrate the raid that took the bridge down. They're out to get him."

"I'd like to have been there," Moshe said, laughing outright. "Don't you know that those Krauts were surprised."

"I'm sure they were," Israel said, enjoying a belly laugh along with his brothers.

The news of the explosion ran though the ghetto the next day like a wildfire, setting off jubilation among the prisoners. Their celebration was short-lived. Chaim's recapture and public execution a few days later was a grim reminder to those remaining, quickly quashing the escape plans of several others. They returned to the daily struggle of the work routines, their unhappiness temporarily eased only by the comfort of seeing their families still intact at day's end.

While the women were always in a struggle, trying to busy themselves with making meals from scraps of food, the few children soon overcame their fear and began to race each other down the street again or took turns playing with a stick, rolling a tire rim up and down the street, dodging furniture as they went. They even shocked the adults by strutting around like soldiers pretending to fire sticks at each other while playing war, an activity that was quickly discouraged.

Laibale was standing by the front door a few days after the selection when a group of young boys, four or five abreast carrying rims and other metal parts of a bicycle, approached the house. Laibale opened the door and stepped outside, wondering what they could want.

"Hello, Laibale," the oldest one said nervously.

"Hello, boys. What are you up to?"

Laibale's smile seemed to dispel their hesitation. A second boy held up a bicycle chain. "We were wondering if you could help us fix this," he said.

Laibale looked at the bedraggled chain silently.

The first boy added, "We found some old bicycle parts." He turned to his friends and encouraged them to show the other objects they were holding. Laibale looked at them with interest but still said nothing. The boy continued, "We thought that maybe, since you're such a good mechanic, you could help us put it together."

Laibale couldn't help but grin at the boys' hope, remembering how he got started building bicycles himself as a youngster. Only a child could see promise in the bent and broken pieces each boy gingerly cradled. Laibale took the chain, turned it over in his hands, and ran his fingers down the interlocking sections, finding the weak links. The boys exchanged excited glances.

"Well, I don't know," Laibale said. "Let me see what else you have here." He got down on his knees and invited them to spread out their treasures.

All the boys dropped to their knees and emptied their pockets, dumping a variety of screws and parts they had collected.

Laibale began to assemble the pieces into a makeshift bicycle pattern. He knew that all motorized vehicles had been forbidden to Jews, and the few bicycles that were allowed were strictly reserved for adults. As the bikes wore out and the tires went flat, what was left of them was simply discarded in a trash pile behind one of the houses. The boys told Laibale that they had discovered the parts while playing hide-and-seek one day.

"These are pretty rough-looking parts," Laibale began. "I don't know." He scratched his head and saw the boys' faces drop in despair.

"But," he continued, "I might be able to patch something together. Give me a few days to see what I can get from the garage. A little grease will do wonders for this chain."

The boys' faces lit up again with anticipation. He added, "You realize that if I can put a bike together, you'll have to keep it hidden."

"Yes, sir," said the first boy with conviction. "We've been hiding these parts for a long time, just waiting until we thought we had enough to bring to you."

Laibale laughed at their determination. "Go ahead home now," he said, patting first one then the other on his back. "I'll do my best."

They started to walk off together, as Laibale picked up the various parts. The first boy ran back and said, "We knew you would help us, Laibale," the boy said his face wide with a smile. "You're the best mechanic anybody has ever seen. You proved that when you won the race in the market square."

"Well, that was a long time ago," Laibale replied, a smile of his own playing around his mouth in appreciation for the memory. "I'll try not to let you down. Go on home now before your parents start to worry about you."

The boys ran off together, racing each other down the street. Laibale took a deep breath and resolved to put that bike together, whatever it took. It was a rare day to see hope in the ghetto. As he leaned down to look at the pile of parts again, he laughed outright when he heard the boys making loud noises, pretending to be motorcycle racers.

Laibale sensed the need they all felt for hope and comfort. He made a conscious effort to be more thoughtful, even when he didn't feel like it. He tried to help the older residents and went out of his way to assist the women by carrying water from the wells to the various houses. One night he quietly suggested that some of them visit the old ones in a show of support, although it was obvious that they'd be taken sooner or later.

The aged ones would often reminisce about their earlier lives, hoping someone would remember their stories and live to recount the family history to their descendants. Each night, as he listened to the stories, Laibale watched in awe as his mother worked feverishly. After having worked all day shoveling coal, she still worked hard at the house trying to patch together clothes for the men required to work at the airport and in other outside brigades.

Like his mother, Laibale felt sorry for the men. They had suffered so much. Many of these men had lost toes and fingers to frostbite, but still they reported to duty every morning just the same. There was no longer any medical attention. The Nazis had announced that there was a communicable disease in the ghetto. That gave them license to nail shut the hospital doors and burn it to the ground with all the patients and medical personnel inside, as well as many orphans who had been given safety there. Laibale was amazed that when no further inhumanity seemed possible, it surfaced anyway.

But then things improved a bit. Laibale thought the Germans must have sensed a need for a diversion from the daily horrors. So they slightly reduced their restrictions at the gate, pretending to be unaware when food was slipped inside or traded through the fence. Much to the prisoners' surprise, some days they even allowed visitors. Laibale was jubilant to return from work one evening and find Father John sitting in the house talking with his mother.

Laibale smiled and Father John rose to greet him. "Why, Laibale, I believe you've grown a few inches since I last saw you." He pumped his hand with a firm handshake.

Laibale's mother chuckled. "If that's true, it's either from eating air or from sheer *chutzpah*," she said, causing all of them to laugh. "We're certainly not getting any extra food rations. Look, Laibale, Father John has brought us some potatoes and a piece of lamb. We'll eat like kings tonight."

"It's a small thing, Nese," Father John said, quietly waving off her praise with an uplifted hand. "I've tried to bring you food several times before, but this is the first time I've been successful."

Laibale's mother whispered her reply. "Do you know what they've done, Father?" She looked over her shoulder, then walked quickly to the door to see if anyone was near before she continued. "You know they're killing us off, don't you?"

The sadness showed in Father John's face. "It's not only you. I understand they have killed all the children in the two closest ghettos as well." He sat silently for a moment, then shrugged weakly. He beckoned Laibale closer with his hand.

Laibale leaned down as Father John whispered, "Is it too late? Do you think you can get the motorcycle to me now?"

"Yes, Father, I can. At least, I think I can." Laibale tried to hide the excitement in his voice. "I'm not sure how quick it will be, though. Sometimes Peter is able to bring me food and medicine for the old ones, but we have to be especially careful. He'd be shot if the guards caught him. I never know exactly when he is coming. I just go to the fence when I can and hope he's there."

"All right. Tell Peter to take his time and just be careful. If it's discovered that we're helping you, I don't have to tell you what will happen to both of us. When he comes, make sure it's at night. Tell him not to even come to my door. I've left a shovel beside the church, stuck deep in the ground. When he hides the bike, tell him to take the shovel out of the dirt and lay it down beside the church. I don't even want to know where he hides the motorcycle. That way, I couldn't confess, even if they tortured me."

Struggling not to show his emotions, Laibale said, "Father, I wish I could do something for you in return."

"You can, Laibale, you can" he replied. "Help your mother. That will be payment enough."

Laibale choked back his emotions. "Thank you again, Father."

"It's not necessary," Father John replied. "Your mother is my friend and I want to help if I can. I will pray for your safety."

Father John stood to leave, saying that he had several others to visit. There were a few Catholics in the ghetto, Laibale knew, incarcerated there because they had offered aid to their Jewish friends. Father John told Laibale that a bribe to one of the guards had only bought him a little time to visit his former parishioners. He hugged Laibale's mother and then squeezed Laibale's shoulder before leaving hurriedly.

As soon as Father John left, Laibale began envisioning a plan of how to move the motorcycle to the church. For the first time in months, he went to bed that night with hope in his heart. He actually looked forward to the new day.

14

Escape Plan

Laibale and his brothers used every spare moment thinking of how Laibale might get outside the ghetto and then return without being detected.

At night, after everyone had gone to bed, Laibale would make his way to Israel and Moshe. Huddled together, they would whisper encouragement to each other. They became so excited with anticipation that they felt almost drunk with the idea of freedom. One night, just for fun, they came up with the outrageous idea of a plan to collect chamber pots from several houses and pour the contents on the sidewalks the guards took when they made their rounds.

"That would teach 'em to keep Jews off the sidewalks," Laibale said.

"Yeah," Moshe added, "We should dump the cans right after one round so it would have time to freeze before the next pass."

In a fit of laughter, Israel said, "I can hear the cussing now, when they step in it.

"Or slip and fall," added Laibale.

The idea of turning their guards into stupid buffoons with such a simple plan sent them into fits of laughter so loud that they woke the others, who joined in the fun. It was wonderful to laugh with abandon and think of living free once again.

But weeks of planning still left them without a foolproof escape idea. Although it was dangerous to trust anyone outside their family, they decided to enlist one of Israel's good friends, Meck.

"Meck might just be the one to help," Israel said. "His mother and sister were herded off to Fort IX just a few days ago. Meck is desperate to see if there's a way to escape this hellhole. I'll go see him tonight."

But only a few hours later, Israel ran back into the house shouting, "Laibale, they've got Meck!"

"What?" Laibale asked.

"They've got him, I tell you. I went to his house and it was empty. His neighbors said he had been dragged off last night, that he had gone crazy when he found out that his girlfriend had been arrested and charged with prostitution. God knows how he did it, but Meck got a pistol. He must have just gone insane! The neighbors said he was running around saying he was going to kill all the bastards."

They were all shaken by the news, and there was no escape plan meeting that night. Early the next morning, the guards arrived, screaming that a collective formation was to be held immediately. No one was to be excluded. Everyone scrambled to dress, knowing that showing up late was always followed by a beating.

Laibale and his brothers arrived at the edge of the crowd, not understanding why the whole ghetto was called to gather so suddenly. They heard the collective gasp before they saw the gallows. Meck's body swung from a rope, still jerking as he strangled to death. It was a strong reminder of what would happen if there was resistance.

Laibale moved closer to his brother and lightly placed his arm around Israel's shoulders. "I'm so sorry," Laibale said, as they watched their friend's life slip away. Israel stiffened to fight back tears. "One thing is for damn sure," he finally got out. "He won't have to dig any more ditches at the airport."

The following day the news came back to the ghetto that Meck's mother, sister, and girlfriend had been immediately executed as retaliation for his actions.

Laibale volunteered to take Meck's place on the dreaded airport detail. If he hoped to get out, he needed to see the surrounding area so that, when the time came, he'd know where he was going. As regrettable as Meck's death was, it had come at a time when Laibale's work in the garage had slowed down. It gave him the perfect reason to volunteer, saying he wanted to work outside in the sunshine for a change. The first day Laibale stood in Meck's place, he made a silent vow to tell Meck's story once he was free.

Meck's body hung on display until the next day. When Laibale walked beside it going to the airport, he saw everything through new eyes. He noticed where the sun rose, where every tree grew, and where every bend in the road was located. Laibale walked with a renewed determination. There was no question that he would escape. The only questions remaining were how and when.

15

Laibale's Luck Changes

The monotony of the airport detail sometimes made Laibale wish he had never volunteered to take Meck's place, especially when it rained for days. Not only did his clothes get soaked after a week of rain, but he felt that his soul was mildewing along with his shirt and trousers.

Some days they worked so late that there was no chance for his boots to dry by the next morning. When he tried to shove his sore feet inside the misshapen leather, the blisters that had formed the day before tore open. There were times that, after the work detail had cleared the guard and left the ghetto, Laibale removed his boots and walked barefoot to the airport. Sometimes the guards forced them to run, while they rode alongside them on bicycles, hurling insults. Even though Laibale tried to avoid the small rocks in the road, they tore open still more sores on his feet. When the pain became so great he thought another step was impossible, the memory of Meck's body swinging slowly from a rope gave him strength to go on.

There had been little talk of escape lately. Meck's execution had produced the desired effect. Frozen fears were plastered on everyone's faces. The men barely spoke among themselves, wanting only to get through the day, return to the ghetto, and see if their families were still alive. The monotonous routine actually provided a sort of peaceful structure to their lives. As long as they didn't break any of the ridiculous rules, plodded to work and back, ate their meager rations, and fell into bed, they seemed safe. At night, though, they could hear an occasional bird singing, assuring them that, although their bodies and minds were in misery, there was life outside the ghetto.

Late one afternoon, as Laibale and Moshe worked near a ditch, Laibale whispered, "Moshe, look what I found." His hands shaking with excitement, Laibale pushed the tip of his shovel under a pair of wire cutters encased in mud. He upended his shovel at his brother's feet and stepped in front of him, standing close enough to guard their secret.

"How do you suppose they got here?" Moshe asked. He knelt to poke through the mud with his fingers, unable to hide his excitement at such an unexpected discovery. He glanced over his shoulder to be sure no guard was watching. "They don't look too old, either."

"Somebody was trying to hide them, no doubt. They just didn't know I'd find them first."

Laibale quickly wiped the grimy cutters on his pants and shoved them inside one of his boots, knowing he would have to find another way to transport them. His feet were so sore that he couldn't bear to walk back to the ghetto like that, and his clothes were so wet that any bulge would be obvious.

But for the moment, feeling the cold metal against his ankle gave Laibale new energy. He shoveled twice as hard the rest of the day, making sure he didn't draw attention to himself by falling behind.

As they lined up for their march back to the ghetto, Moshe and Laibale exchanged knowing glances. Laibale removed his boots, leaving the cutters inside. He couldn't risk leaving them behind. When he approached the ghetto, he was relieved to see one of the more humane guards standing at the main gate. Without waiting to be asked, Laibale held his arms above his head for the body search, the boots suspended in air. He simply explained that he had blisters on his feet and was trying to save them for the next day's work. It seemed the guard almost smiled before he waved Laibale inside the gates.

Israel couldn't believe Laibale's good luck.

"It seems you're destined to leave our glorious estate," Israel said, laughing and spreading his hands to encompass their tiny living quarters. He grew quiet and touched Laibale's shoulder gently. "If any of us make it to the outside, it will be you."

Israel's uncharacteristic emotion made Laibale uncomfortable. He stepped aside. "I'm going to walk the fence tonight," he said. "There has to be a weak link somewhere. If it exists, I'll find it."

Later, in the dark, Laibale could feel the adrenaline rising as he waited for a chance to get outside, especially since there had been a break in the rain that day. He knew he would have to find a spot that wasn't easily visible from the guard towers, as it would take several minutes to get through the barbed wire and then restore it. He carefully slipped in and out of shadows until he found a back corner that faced Paneriu Street.

"Perfect," he thought. "I want to go down the street where so many Jews have been marched to their death. This Jew is going to live."

On his return to the house, he also mulled over what he had heard about a new shipment of motorcycle parts arriving that day. He was certain he would be called back to the garage to start the repair work. That fit perfectly into his plan, as he had a supply of wire there. He would need some of it to patch the fence, once he was on the other side.

16

Nese Needs Medicine

The continuing rain and dampness began affecting everyone, especially Laibale's mother. She had been on the thin side all her life and plagued with allergies and asthma for most of it. She always sneezed a lot at springtime, but now, in the autumn, she had trouble breathing as the weather turned cool and the leaves started falling.

She had been treated for tuberculosis once a long time ago, and after several months away one summer, she came back looking rested. After that, summer was always her favorite time of year. Now, though, she was always tired. She struggled to breathe and needed the medication she usually got each time the seasons changed.

"Mama, you're coughing more than usual," Laibale said one night when they stood in the kitchen. She seemed to ignore him at first and just kept stirring a pot of soup she was making from potato peelings.

"This soup is so weak, it probably won't even taste like potatoes," she said, with a look of disgust on her face. Then she brightened, laughed, and added, "Maybe we should count our blessings. I'm told the peelings are where the real nourishment is anyway. I guess we should just be thankful that the Nazis let us have them."

Laibale didn't respond or walk away from her. After a short silence, she patted Laibale's arm and said, "Oh, Laibale, don't fret over me so." Laibale moved closer to his mother and put his arm around her waist, giving her a little hug. "I'm just getting older, that's all," she said. "Not having my medicine has made it worse, but I'll feel better when it stops raining so much. I always feel better in the spring. Once I get past the pollen, I can count on the birds to cheer me up."

Laibale made a silent vow to get the medication somehow. It could be had, he knew, for a price. His determination grew after he took special care to watch his mother on a daily basis. She had begun to look even more frail and she coughed almost constantly, especially at night. Laibale's concern turned to alarm when he saw her one morning, bent forward and spent from coughing. She did her best to compose herself when she realized he was watching her.

"I'm so sorry, Mama," Laibale said, his voice breaking. He put his arms around her to steady her as another wave of coughing started. Unable to speak, she gasped for breath. As she leaned on him, he felt the thinness of her body, usually shrouded in an old dress and a sweater, through her nightclothes. Laibale felt the bones in her back as he hugged her and realized that, unless something were done immediately, he would lose her to malnutrition and overwork, the same fate so many others had met.

Later that night, Laibale whispered in Israel's ear. "I'm going out."

"What?" his brother asked from a half-asleep stupor. "Where are you going?"

"To get Mama some medicine. I've sent word to the

pharmacist that I would meet him just after midnight. I didn't tell Mama. It would just worry her."

"How are you going to pay for it?"

"I dug Mama's necklace out of the wall. You know, the one she has been keeping in case of an emergency. What good will it do us if she dies? Besides that, it's her jewelry. It ought to be used to keep her alive."

Now fully awake and frightened for his little brother, Israel reached out and hugged Laibale fiercely. "I know better than to try to change your mind. Please be careful. If anything happens to you, Mama will hold me accountable, since I knew you were going out."

"Don't you worry. I'll be back before daylight."

Laibale lay down for another hour, making sure he had allowed enough time for the guards to complete one of their shift changes. When the sound of the jackboots finally faded, he slipped silently to the door, passing beside Israel on the way out. His brother raised a hand to stop him momentarily. Their fingers touched briefly and then Laibale melted into the blackness like a cat.

He edged along the street, tiptoeing and pressing his body as closely to the buildings as he dared. He stopped and listened often, discerning every sound, even the snores coming from the houses before making his way to Paneriu Street. Finally he found the corner with the slack spot in the fence, deftly cut the wire, and stepped through. He snagged his hand when a barb caught him, almost causing him to curse out loud. He wiped the blood on his pants and quickly repaired the hole with the wire he had stolen from the garage. He smiled into the darkness, congratulating himself for his cleverness. Practically giddy with success, he took a deep breath and steadied himself before making his way to the appointed meeting place.

Laibale saw the figure in the shadows before he could make out his face. It was a relief when the pharmacist spoke.

"I thought you were coming earlier," he hissed.

"I got out as soon as I could. Do you have it?"

"Why do you think I'm here, to meet a woman?" the pharmacist snorted.

Laibale could sense the disgust on the man's face as he traded his mother's necklace for the bottle of pills.

"Tell her to take only one a day for about a week, until her body adjusts to it again," the man said, his voice softening a little. "After that, she can take one in the morning and one at night. This should be enough to hold her until the weather clears. After that, she'll breathe easier."

"I can't thank you enough," Laibale said.

"You can thank me by getting out of here," the pharmacist replied. "I won't do this again, you hear. Tell your mother that I've now paid for that wedding dress she made for my daughter. Don't be sending me any more messages."

Laibale stood gripping the bottle of pills, overjoyed that he had accomplished what had been thought impossible. All he had to do now was get back inside the ghetto.

He retraced his path as fast as he dared. He had just a few minutes before there would be a bed check. The most vicious guards often flung open the doors to the houses, shining torchlights around, making sure there were no empty beds. Once, when it was discovered that a man was missing, they shot everyone who was left in the house. The guards were waiting for the man when he tried to sneak back in, following a visit with a girlfriend. They roped him and his girlfriend back to back and shot them with a single bullet the next morning, forcing the work brigades to march by the bleeding bodies.

As Laibale neared his escape hole in the fence, he heard a voice whisper his name. Laibale whirled around, clutching the medicine to his chest, and realized his friend Peter was standing in the dark.

Laibale feared he would faint from relief. "Peter, what are you doing here?"

"I've been coming every night for a week, hoping to catch you. I saw Father John at confession and he said you had something to tell me."

"I've been wondering how I would get a message to you about the motorcycle," Laibale said. He spoke quickly, giving instructions to Peter about hiding his motorcycle at the priest's home and how to leave the shovel on the ground.

Laibale feared for Peter. He asked, "Are you sure you still want to do this? It's a terrible risk."

"It's all right. You'd do the same for me."

The friends hurriedly embraced, then parted. Laibale made his way back into the ghetto without incident.

"I'm back," he whispered, leaning down to speak into Israel's ear.

"Did you get it?" Israel asked.

"Well, I didn't go to meet a woman," Laibale said, borrowing the pharmacist's retort. Sensing Israel's smile, he poked his brother's side with his finger and crawled into bed with his clothes on. He would only have a couple of hours to rest and didn't want to waste any of it on redressing. He held the bottle of pills in one hand near his side, secure in the knowledge that he had bought some precious time for his mother. He reveled in the risk that Peter had taken and in the thought of escape.

17

A Welcome Respite

Laibale was too excited to fall asleep. He hadn't felt so victorious since the day he won the race. It had been two years since they entered Kovno Ghetto, and the joy of crossing the finish line in first place had almost vanished, replaced with the continuous tragedy of daily life.

When dawn began to break, Laibale couldn't control his anxious legs any longer. He crept over to his mother's bed and knelt beside it. He watched her steady breathing for a moment, hesitating to interrupt her rest. After a few minutes passed, she stirred slightly, giving him the courage to gently touch her shoulder.

"I'm so tired," she said, not fully conscious. "It can't be time to get up yet."

"You'll want to get up when you see what I have for you," Laibale whispered.

"Laibale! What's wrong?" His mother said with a jolt.

"Nothing is wrong. For a change, everything is right." Laibale held up the bottle of pills for her to see.

"Where did you get this? What have you done?" She sat up and pushed Laibale's arm away so she could see the medicine better. She was now fully awake and both frightened for the peril the medicine would cause if discovered and the joy of having it once again. "Where did you get this?" she asked again, a smile slowly moving across her face.

"I got them at the getting place," Laibale said with a laugh, knowing that his mother would rejoice that he had fooled the dreaded guards once again. Laibale's mother laughed but then turned serious.

"These had to come from a pharmacist," she said, touching the bottle in disbelief. "They must have cost a fortune. Did you trade your rations for them?"

"Well, you might say I traded a strand of gold for a heart of gold. Now stop asking questions and sit up. I'll get you some water so you can take one."

The commotion had wakened the others, who gathered around Laibale's mother in utter disbelief. Israel began strutting around and telling the story of how Laibale surprised him just before leaving the ghetto, taking obvious delight in holding everyone's attention. He emphasized how he had cautioned Laibale to be careful.

"I took your advice seriously, big brother," Laibale added. "I was outside that fence before you could blink. Those wire cutters sure came in handy."

Their mother was even more confused. "Wire cutters? What wire cutters?"

"Some things are better left unsaid," Laibale replied. He pulled her to her feet. "Now, how about if you get dressed and I'll make you some breakfast? Cooking will be easy after mending fences. I've worked up quite an appetite."

For days afterward the family exchanged knowing glances and subdued smiles, reveling in their secret. They all stood a bit taller and more erect, walked with a purpose. They were now more confident as they basked in the hope for a real escape.

Laibale eventually told his mother how he had exchanged her necklace for the medicine. At first she was dismayed, as the necklace had been a birthday gift from her three boys when they were very young. But she felt so much better from the medicine that she couldn't argue with the decision.

Soon the weather turned warmer and life returned to the trees. The medicine had acted as the buffer that Laibale's mother had needed, and she felt even better, especially when she heard birds singing.

Before long, the demand for more factory workers increased, as it did from time to time. Up to that point, some of the women had been spared. The few who were privileged enough to prepare meals in the kitchen had worked out a way to take turns caring for each other's children. On rare occasions, a few children went with their mothers to work. Some of the Germans who guarded the ghetto actually enjoyed seeing them play on the floors as they ate, giving them a break from their grim duties. Now, though, there was a sudden call for sewing machine operators. More uniforms were needed for the Germans on the battlefront, and additional workers were being added to accommodate the demand.

"Moshe, did you see the notice directing all the women to report to the sewing factory?" Laibale asked his brother.

"I just heard about it," Moshe spat. "I don't know how to tell Sheina. She'll go crazy because she will have to leave Sara."

"Tell her about the Brownsteins. They managed to bribe a Catholic couple who got false papers for their little girl to get out. I hear the Brownsteins even got word that she was being well cared for."

"Well, I'm not a Brownstein," Moshe growled. "You know the Gillmans don't have any money."

"I just hope they aren't planning another selection," Laibale said quietly. "Father John said they're culling out the children in all the ghettos."

"How can you say that, Laibale?" Moshe's face was ashen. With tears forming in his eyes, he said, "I'd gladly give my life for Sara, but it's worthless here. I don't have anything to trade."

"Yes. I know all that," Laibale said, "but you know how Mama always said that nothing beats a failure but a try. Well, I might fail but I'm going to try. Let me think on it for a while."

"Sara is just a baby still," Moshe said, pacing. "She doesn't understand how to be quiet. You know she nearly got us all killed with her crying at the big selection."

"I know that, too," Laibale said, his voice determined. "Be that as it may, I can't just stand by and let them kill her. She is our only hope for the future."

18

Sheina and Sara

Sheina was inconsolable when she learned of her new work assignment.

Moshe asked Laibale to try to talk with her about giving up Sara. He had also asked his mother to take Sara for a walk so that Sara would not overhear the conversation. He was afraid Sheina might get hysterical.

When Sheina was washing the supper dishes, Laibale took a deep breath. "Sheina, I've been thinking about Sara and how we've been lucky to keep her alive this long," he began. "Now that you can't be with her much, with your new work assignment and all." His voice faltered. "Well, we just have to think of a plan to save her."

Sheina didn't say anything. She started drying the dishes. Laibale took another breath and started again. "Did you hear about how the Brownsteins were able to get their daughter out? A Catholic couple has her."

Sheina turned toward him, her eyes shooting fire. "I'd rather kill her than send her away."

Moshe spoke up. "Sheina, you're not making sense. We have to try." He stood and walked around the kitchen table, then placed his hands on his wife's shoulders. "What if there is another selection? Laibale says he heard they are killing all the children in the Vilna Ghetto and that's just a few miles from here. Maybe we could find a nice Catholic family."

"A nice family? A nice Catholic family?" Sheina nearly screamed, her eyes wild with fear. "Ask Ruth Davidovich about nice. Ruth's husband, Simeon, told me just yesterday that he went to the fence to trade. Ruth is terribly sick and she wanted some real butter one more time before she died. Their anniversary was yesterday, so Simeon traded his extra coat for a pound of butter. He ran home without even unwrapping the package to surprise Ruth. Her surprise turned out to be a brick. That was from a nice Catholic family."

"Sheina, Sheina," Moshe cajoled. "That was butter. This is our child." We have to try something to save her. You know how many children have already been killed." Then he added, "She's our only child."

"Do you think I'm *meshuggah*?" Sheina asked shrilly. "Do you have to tell me she's our only child? I'm the one who brought her into this world, but the Germans will kill her if she gets out and they discover that she is a Jew. I won't agree, I tell you."

Laibale spoke up, his voice tender. "We can't wait, Sheina. There hasn't been a selection in a long time. You know what that means. None of us wants to send her away, but if we don't act now, we may not have the chance."

He stepped away so the couple could talk. Moshe continued his pleading. Sheina turned her back and walked out into the hallway. Moshe followed her, still urging her to reconsider. Sheina sobbed and grabbed her hair with both hands, pulling hard in distress. She finally collapsed into Moshe's arms.

"All right, Moshe," she said with a muffled sob. "You win,

but you have to be the one to arrange it. I cannot bear it."

Moshe did his best to wipe his wife's tears, while fighting back his own. Laibale quietly walked to the doorway. "I know it's very hard on you," Laibale said. He touched Sheina gently on the shoulder and stood quietly for a moment, then turned to his brother.

"Let's go for a walk," he suggested. "You never know if these walls have ears."

"You're the one with the biggest ears around here," Moshe said, pulling one of Laibale's earlobes. They were both relieved at a chance to laugh.

The two men left Sheina holding her head and sitting at the kitchen table.

When they were a safe distance from the house, Laibale said, "Sara may be the last child in our family. If we have a future, it's through her."

"Yes," Moshe agreed, nodding his head. "I can't stand the thought of her dying so young. So we have to find a way, Laibale. We have to."

"I know. I know. Maybe Father John can help."

That night, Laibale made his way out of the ghetto again, hoping to find help from their Catholic friend. He had completed the repairs to the barbed wire when he heard the guard approaching. He dropped to his stomach and used his elbows to inch away from the fence. He crawled farther into the darkness, his heart pounding in his ears, and held his breath until the guard passed. As he finally breathed, he realized that, in his distress over Sara, he had miscalculated the time for the inspection rounds. He silently scolded himself. He knew that if anyone discovered him on the outside perimeter, he and his whole family would be shot.

19

Father John

Laibale stood in the dark at Father John's back door and knocked softly. After a moment, he saw the light of a candle.

Father John opened the door a few inches, just enough to see him.

He snuffed out the candle quickly. "Laibale, what are you doing here?" he asked.

"I'm desperate, Father John, or I wouldn't have come."

"Hurry! Get inside. Go to my study. It's down the hall, the last door on the right. I don't dare turn on any lights. There's a closet just inside the door, on the left. Stay there until I come."

Laibale stumbled into a table, barely catching it before it clattered to the floor, then made his way through the dark house, feeling along the wall until he found the door opening. He made his way into the room and slipped inside the closet. He strained his ears to hear Father John. The priest stayed on the porch for a long time. He must have been listening and peering into the darkness, trying to decide whether Laibale had been followed.

After a long while, Father John entered the study. He lit a stubby candle and sat at his desk. He opened his Bible and began to read aloud.

"The Lord is my shepherd; I shall not want. He maketh me to lie down in green pastures. He leadeth me beside the still waters. He restoreth my soul. He leadeth me in paths of righteousness for his name's sake."

Father John picked up the Bible and walked slowly around the room, still reading aloud but with a quieter tone. "Yea, though I walk through the valley of the shadow of death, I will fear no evil, for thou art with me. Thy rod and thy staff they comfort me."

Then he whispered, "Speak quickly, Laibale." He walked back and forth a few feet in front of the closet.

"Can you save my brother's child, if I can get her to you?"

"How old is she?"

"Almost three, I think."

"Ah, just a baby. I don't know, Laibale."

The priest raised his voice and began reading again. "Thou preparest a table before me in the presence of my enemies. Thou anointest my head with oil; my cup runneth over. Surely goodness and mercy shall follow me all the days of my life, and I will dwell in the house of the Lord forever."

Quiet returned as the priest walked slowly back to the closet.

"Bring her in two nights," he whispered.

"But, Father John, what will do you with her?"

"I always visit the nunnery on Friday morning. I'll take her to the sisters. They're already hiding other Jewish children. The nuns have ways of protecting them. Wait at least a half hour until I have left the room. Go out the way you came."

"God bless you, Father."

"And, you, my child."

Father John walked around a while longer, continuing to read aloud. He began to yawn and stretch. He blew out the candle and sat in the darkness while Laibale quietly turned the knob on the back door and slipped out.

Laibale hurried as fast as he could back to the fence. This time he unfurled the barbed wire carefully, to avoid more cuts on his hands. Just as he began to unwind the wire, a dog barked. Laibale dropped to his belly and froze, afraid the guards might be searching the perimeter with a German shepherd, something they did when they believed a prisoner was missing.

Another dog barked, louder and more furiously than the first, setting off a foray of growls and yelps that escalated into a pitched frenzy. Laibale tried not to breathe. When one of the dogs whimpered and a soldier laughed, Laibale realized the guards had been pitting their dogs against each other to see who had the fiercest one.

Finally, quiet surrounded Laibale. He got to his knees and worked quickly to close the gaping fence. He slipped away just before the guard changed for the last time that night. He quietly entered his house and lay down on his bed without even undressing. He knew what hard work was ahead of him. Somehow he had to convince Sheina that Sara would be safer outside the ghetto. Even more difficult would be finding the strength to get her out.

20

Sara's Departure

U nable to sleep, Laibale rose very early and made his way to his mother's bed. He hated to wake her but he needed to talk with her. Sara was her only grandchild. Laibale and his mother had often spoken of how Sara could, somehow, carry on the family history, should the rest of them die in the ghetto. None of them could have ever dreamed that vast numbers of Jewish children would be murdered nor could they imagine that they would be plotting to save Sara by giving her away

"Mama," he said gently.

"Laibale, what's wrong?" his mother asked, half asleep.

"I need you to help me."

"Can't it wait until morning?" she asked with some aggravation. She sighed. "No, if you're waking me, I guess it can't."

She sat up on the side of the bed and made room for him to sit down beside her. Together they exchanged whispers about the plan. Finally, Laibale's mother supported the decision to send Sara away immediately.

When morning came, Sheina stood at the stove, stirring the gruel they had each day for breakfast. She tried to keep her tears from falling into the pot. She had bribed another woman to work in her place so she could spend the whole day with Sara.

"Sara loves oatmeal," Sheina said out loud to the others, stopping to wipe her eyes with her apron. "But all we have is this slop. It was bad enough before they cut the rations. I'll write a note to put in the sack. Whoever reads it will know that her favorite breakfast is oatmeal and honey. Maybe they still have honey."

Laibale's mother tried to comfort her daughter-in-law. "I'm sure the nuns have honey," she said.

Laibale lied his way out of working and came back to the house in the late afternoon, afraid that Sheina would change her mind. He tried to be inconspicuous, as Sheina prepared for the inevitable. He watched from his bedroom door as Sara perched on the sink by her mother, singing little songs that Sheina usually sang to her at bedtime. She was unaware of the finality of it all. She helped hang her two extra dresses and two pairs of panties on the drying rack that Sheina had washed to send along with her. They would dry by nightfall.

Later, when it was time for Sara's nap, Laibale said, "I'll watch her for you." Sheina tucked Sara into bed, taking extra time to tell her a story about how a little girl who had gone on an adventure with her favorite uncle to a new home. When Sara fell asleep, Laibale sat beside her. He looked at her innocent face and wondered if he would ever see her again. Sheina went about gathering things to send with her daughter. She wiped off Sara's shoes. Since she only had one pair, she would be wearing them.

Laibale saw Sheina hold up the tiny coat that Laibale's mother had made. It was almost threadbare now. Sheina turned to her mother-in-law. "Can you re-sew these buttons?"

Her voice cracked again.

"Of course," Laibale's mother replied. She took the coat, went to her sewing basket, and worked quickly. Once the buttons were secure, she buried her face in the coat, breathing in her only grandchild's scent.

There were no toys to send along. Sara always entertained everyone at night by making her own toys out of kitchen spoons. She chattered nonsensically, although she was easy to understand. She had learned to speak very early, her childhood swallowed up by the daily ghetto routine. One night she had arranged the cooking pots and declared to the whole family that they now lived on a farm. She could not understand why everyone laughed so hard when she sat down on one of the pots and said she had to milk the cow so they would have milk for breakfast.

The hands on the clock seemed to fly. Sensing Sheina's anxiety, Laibale woke Sara from her nap, rationalizing it by thinking that less sleep now would make her extra tired that night when she needed to sleep. Sheina spent the rest of the day holding Sara in her lap, singing all her favorite songs, and making finger puppets on the wall.

Laibale was standing in the doorway when Moshe returned from work, stepped inside, and stooped down as he did every evening. When Sara heard his voice, she ran and jumped into his arms. "Papeh! Papeh! I missed you!"

Laibale fought to hold back tears as he watched. Sheina turned her back as well. Laibale knew that Moshe was also fighting for control.

Night had already begun to fall. Laibale's mother set the table. Sheina moved quickly, writing the note and putting it into the sack and then, with deliberate slowness, rearranged the bowls several times before calling everyone to the table. From the stove, she turned to look at Moshe and nodded. That was their pre-arranged signal that Sheina was ready to add the last tablespoon of honey they had, along with paregoric, a bit of sleep-inducing medicine, to Sara's soup. That way she would be asleep when Laibale was ready to leave.

Sara ate her soup with gusto and licked the spoon her mother handed her, enjoying the last bit of the honey. Soon thereafter, her head began to nod. She cupped her hands, forming a makeshift pillow, and rested her head on the table. Moshe lifted her and sat holding her to his chest until Laibale finished eating and stood up.

"It's time, brother," Laibale said. "I'll wait outside."

Moshe placed Sara in Sheina's lap a final time. He knelt on the floor beside them, encircling both of them with his arms for a few minutes. Without a word, he gently lifted Sara and cradled her to his chest again, squeezing her gently. At the door, he turned and looked at Sheina. She rose to hand him the sack. Neither of them could speak. Laibale left first and Moshe followed him through the door.

Laibale walked just in front of Moshe and quickly unfurled the barbed wire. Without a word, Moshe handed Sara and the sack of belongings to Laibale. It had been decided earlier that Laibale would leave immediately and Moshe would mend the fence.

Moshe said a prayer for his only child, and another for Laibale's courage, then turned his attention to the hole in the fence.

It was almost dawn before Laibale returned. He stooped to whisper into Moshe's ear. "Your prayers have been answered."

21

Surprise Search

The sun hadn't fully risen when a Nazi guard threw open the door. He screamed, "*Schnell! Schnell!* Fast! Fast! Everybody outside!"

Half asleep, still in their nightclothes and terrified, Laibale and his family were forced to line up and stand at attention to be counted. The huge Nazi strode back and forth in front of them, as other families were routed from their slumber.

"I thought there was a child in this family," the guard snarled, stopping right in front of Moshe.

"We had a daughter," Moshe replied. "She died yesterday."

"Why didn't you report this? You know we have to have an accurate count."

"Yes, I was going to tell you today. Our tradition demands that we bury before sundown." Moshe held up both hands and shrugged in mock exasperation. "She was our only child." Moshe reached for Sheina, who was crying.

"No matter," the soldier said coldly. "One less Jew to count. We're looking for contraband," he said. "We know that someone is getting out of the ghetto. Make no mistake. He will die if we find out who it is."

The guard's attention shifted to a fight that had broken out farther down the line. He ran to help restore order, as Moshe did his best to calm Sheina. Then, just as things grew quiet, Laibale's mother began to cough uncontrollably. Laibale had to steady her, as the coughing grew worse and bent her double, catching the guard's attention again. He walked quickly back to them. "What's the matter with her?" he demanded.

"Oh, it's just a summer cold," Laibale said. "She gets one every year. It will pass in a few days."

He sneered and stepped closer to Laibale's mother. "Well, it better. Sick Jews are dead Jews." Then he walked away.

When the count was finally completed, everyone was allowed to return home to eat before joining the work details leaving the ghetto. The chaos seemed under control for one more day. That evening, after the lights were out, Laibale slipped out of bed and touched Moshe on the shoulder. They crawled to Israel's bed and awakened him.

"What's the matter?" Israel asked groggily.

"It's Mama," Laibale whispered. "Get up. We've got to talk."

"She's getting worse," Moshe added.

"I don't think the medicine is working anymore," Laibale said. "What do you think we ought to do?"

"She's got to have medical attention," Moshe said. "She's getting weaker every day. What do you say, Israel?"

"You're asking me?" Israel replied. "I don't know what to do. Laibale is the one who can get in and out of the ghetto. If she has to go out, he should be the one to take her. If the Nazis discover that they're gone, though, we'll all be shot."

"That's a chance we have to take," Laibale said. "She's our mother. I'd rather die for her than die because a damn Nazi doesn't like the way I walk."

"But where will you go?" Moshe asked, his voice suddenly fearful.

"Don't worry about it," Laibale replied. "I'll figure something out." He reached to squeeze Moshe's shoulder in the dark. "It's decided then," he added with a sigh of relief. "I'll wait a few days to let things get back to normal before going out. Let's get to bed. There isn't much left of the night."

22

Run For Life

The next three days were calm, although Laibale felt anything but calm. He had hardly slept since he had decided to leave the ghetto with his mother. He realized that, for the first time in his life, he would be leaving his older brothers behind. Although he surely had not always agreed with them, their constant presence had been a mainstay in his life. In a pinch, he could always count on them. If he failed in his escape attempt, it could condemn his entire family to an early grave. He suddenly felt much older than 17.

His mother's coughing had become worse. When Laibale returned from work one day to find her lying on the couch, unable to cook, he knew there was no time to spare. He knelt beside her and shared his escape plan. At first she tried to protest, but then realized there was no other way. After supper, Laibale quietly told Moshe and Israel that they would be gone by morning. They all said their goodbyes before going to bed.

"I don't have to tell you to be careful, brother," Moshe said, his voice breaking with emotion. He hugged Laibale.

"That's right," Israel added, touching Laibale on the elbow. Trying to lighten the moment, he added, "Be extra careful. I've got another brother, but I only have one mother."

"Stop with the worrying, boys," their mother said in a barely audible voice. "We'll be fine. Don't forget that I'll be with the Little Lion."

"I'm sure you will be fine, Mama," Israel said. He hugged her, then sat on the bed and pulled off his shoes and handed them to Laibale.

"Here," he said, his voice cracking slightly. "You'll need to walk fast, something you can't do in those old boots."

"Thanks, Israel," Laibale replied. "These will come in handy." Laibale put the shoes beside his bed, hugged his mother, and lay on top of the covers.

When daylight came, Laibale had left no evidence that he or his mother had ever been in the house, except for the pair of gnarled boots beside his bed.

Although they left in total darkness in order to travel quickly, Laibale's mother was so weak that it hampered their progress. They still hadn't made much headway by daylight. Laibale was terrified they would be discovered before he could get them to a hiding place not far from the ghetto. When they finally reached the abandoned shed, Laibale let her catch her breath while he tried to think of what to do next. His mother obviously couldn't walk very far, and they had little food and water to sustain them. When Moshe had offered extra bread, Laibale had refused, thinking that it would only be wasted if they were caught. Now he wished he had brought it.

Even though his mother's coughing had stopped and she seemed temporarily stronger, her color appeared gray and she had begun to sweat. Laibale was afraid for her to venture any farther for fear she would have a heart attack.

"I'm going to leave you here, Mama," he finally said.

"It's so close to the ghetto. I can walk some more." She tried to struggle to her feet.

"It's too dangerous. I can move quicker without you." Laibale spoke gently. "I promise to come back within a day, you'll see. You just stay still and try not to cough. Here, I'll leave the food and water with you. That should help."

"But what will you do? You can't survive without food or water."

"I'm going to be moving too fast to eat or drink," Laibale said. He grinned at his mother and tweaked her on the chin. "The Little Lion will be on the prowl. Now you try to rest because when I return, we'll have to make a quick getaway."

Relieved and exhausted, his mother slipped into a quiet sleep. Laibale watched her chest rise and fall for a short while and prayed that she would live until he returned. He touched her thin arm a final time and slipped out the side of the shed, quickly making his way to a patch of woods. He darted through the woods, moving farther and farther away. When night fell, he knocked on Father John's back door.

"Who is it?" Father John asked without opening the door.

"It's Laibale Gillman."

Father John opened the door in the darkness.

"Laibale, quickly come in. Get in the closet."

Remembering to avoid the table this time, Laibale practically ran down the hall and took his place in the closet, pulling the priest's extra frocks around him. Father John followed him close behind.

"Laibale, it's good to see that you're alive. I've heard of all the selections." Father John spoke softly. He paused for a moment and then asked, "Does Nese still live?"

"Just barely. That's why I've come. She's hiding in a shed near the ghetto and she is terribly sick. I have to get her to a doctor."

"How do you plan to do that?"

"I'm not sure. I've come for the motorcycle." Laibale paused for a minute trying to gather courage. "You've been so good to us and I hate to ask, but I have no one else to turn to. Can you help us?"

"I'm being watched constantly now," Father John said.

Suddenly lights shown through the window and a man started beating on the door.

"Open up or I'll break the door down!"

"I'm coming. I'm coming," Father John spoke in a loud voice as he opened the door. "What on earth do you want at this time of night, officer?"

"I heard you talking to someone."

"I was at prayer, as I am every evening at this time. So many people need help these days and the day is so full that I seldom have time to contemplate or pray alone. Would you care to join me? How long has it been since you've taken communion?"

"Not long enough. Now get out of my way." He motioned for a second officer to join him.

"Just as you say," Father John said, holding the door wide so the two men could pass. They started opening drawers and flinging things about.

"Here, I'll help you," Father John offered, as he began opening closet doors in the living room.

"Get out of the way, I told you," the first officer said. He pushed past the priest and opened other doors and cabinets even more rapidly, strewing the contents all over the room.

"Go easy, will you? He's just an old man." The second officer spoke up. "My uncle is a priest."

"Well, if you love them so much, you should become one."

"Sometimes I wish I had. It would beat shooting Jews. Come on. There's nobody here but the father."

The arrogant guard walked in front of the priest and purposely pushed into him.

"Luck was on your side this time, old man. The next time he might not be with me." He jerked his thumb toward the other guard. "You'd better watch your step."

"I shall, officer, I shall. Thank you for the warning and may God go with you." He eased the door closed behind them.

Laibale heard Father John go to his altar and pray aloud. He knelt there for a long time to make sure the Nazis had left him in peace. Laibale felt so tired as he waited that he closed his eyes, grateful for the chance to rest. He jerked awake when the priest touched his shoulder. "I wish you could rest, my lad, but you have much ahead of you."

Laibale was still fearful. "Did you get rid of them?"

"Yes, of course."

"How?"

"Divine intervention, my child. Now get up. I'll fix you some food."

As Laibale slipped outside to relieve himself, Father John cut slabs of bread and cheese and placed some of it in a cloth sack. Laibale quickly ate the sandwich the priest had left on the table and gulped down a glass of milk as well. They sat in the darkness, save for a shaft of moonlight through the kitchen window. Father John gave Laibale explicit instructions.

"I cannot help you," he began.

"But Father John, I have to do something." Laibale's voice broke with anxiety. "Mama will die unless she gets to a hospital."

"I understand, Laibale. Let me finish. There is another priest, Father Bruno, who has just moved into the area from Vilnius. It's been rumored that he has Jewish ancestry, but they haven't been able to trace it. He has been removed from his position for now and is waiting for the investigation to be complete. I understand he's living near Slobodka and has developed connections with the partisans. If there is help to be had, it will have to be through Father Bruno."

"Maybe it's a good thing we didn't get too far from the ghetto after all," Laibale said, with a sense of relief.

"Yes, things do seem to have a strange way of working out sometimes," Father John added, reaching to pat Laibale's arm. "Here, take this bag of food. It will tide you over until you get to Father Bruno. Go at night to his bedroom window and knock three times. Wait a few minutes and knock five times. When he comes to the window and raises it, you must tell him the password, *'Zahor.'*"

"But Father, that's the Yiddish word for 'remember,'" Laibale said in disbelief.

"Exactly, my child. Do you think a Nazi would use such a word or even know what it meant?"

Laibale smiled at the explanation. Father John reached out and embraced him quickly.

"And, please tell your dear mother that I pray for her every time I place my cowl over my head and see her fine handwork."

"She'll be glad to know that, Father," Laibale said, his voice thick with emotion. "Thank you again." He crept outside, glad for the darkness.

23

Father Bruno

L aibale recovered his motorcycle, thrilled to know that Peter had been successful in carrying out their plan. Laibale switched on the torchlight he had carried and cupped one hand over the end of it, allowing only a sliver of light for his work. He removed the spark plugs and cleaned them. After a few more adjustments and checks, he was delighted to hear it start on the first attempt.

Congratulating himself on being such a good mechanic, he quickly made his way back to the shed where he had left his mother. He shut off the engine and walked the bike the rest of the way in silence. He hid the bike beside some bushes and went in. His mother was so exhausted that she didn't even rise to see who had come into the shed. Laibale softly said "Mama" and sat down beside her. He gently took her hand.

"Laibale, you're safe."

"Yes, not only safe, but Father John sent you something." Laibale placed the sandwich in her hands.

"Such a good man." She began to stuff huge bites of cheese and bread into her mouth.

"Slow down. You'll choke."

"It's so good. I can't help myself. Remember how you used to eat my *lochen kugel*?"

"Ah, yes. What I wouldn't give to taste it again."

"You will, just as soon as I'm well again."

"Yes, we have to see to that. As soon as you're finished, we're leaving. Father John told me of another priest who is helping the partisans. He lives nearby, not too far from Slobodka."

"What do you mean another priest? Helping partisans? Near Slobodka?" His mother stopped chewing, unable to hide the astonishment in her voice.

"It's a long story. I'll tell you when we get there. Now, see if you can stand up." She made it over to the motorcycle with Laibale's help. He gently steadied her as she swung her leg over the bike. He set out pushing the motorcycle, noticing that his mother's frail weight made little difference in his efforts to move it.

Finally Laibale thought it was safe to start the engine. He mounted the bike in front of her.

"Hold on tight, Mama. There may be some bumps in the road. I don't want to turn the lights on and I can't see much more than how to stay in the road."

"Okay, Laibale. I'll do my best." She held his waist and rested her head on his shoulder with relief.

They traveled for a while until Laibale sensed his mother becoming weak. Her grip loosened around his waist.

"I think we'd better stop and hide for a while," Laibale said. "There's some undergrowth not too far from here."

"We haven't gone very far, have we?" his mother asked.

"Far enough for now, I think."

His mother's silence let Laibale know that she had done

all she could just to stay on the motorcycle. After dismounting, they found a small patch of woods to hide in and ate the last of their food. Laibale's mother had a coughing fit that left her spent. When Laibale tried to rouse her, he realized she just couldn't go on.

"I'll go to Father Bruno's myself," he said quietly. "You just rest. Everything will be all right."

"Be careful, Little Lion."

"I always am. Don't worry."

After what seemed like hours, he arrived at a dirt road, hoping it was the one that led to Father Bruno's house. Looking down the road, Laibale saw another path with three large poplar trees beside it, one of the markers Father John had said to look for. He took the path, which was shielded on either side by more trees, and was relieved when a little white house near a small clearing in the woods came into view. It had green shutters and two flower boxes out front, painted red and hanging from the windows, and there was a vegetable garden beside the house, all things Father John had described. With a deep sigh of relief, Laibale found a place to hide in the woods to await another nightfall.

24

A Stranger Helps

Laibale knocked three times on the window and waited. Then he knocked five times. No one came. He repeated the knocking sequence. Still, no one came. Finally, he leaned down to the window, which was open by a sliver.

"*Zahor.*"

The silence that followed chilled Laibale so much he almost ran.

Finally, a man's voice spoke. "Go to the back."

Laibale ran to the back of the tiny house. Through a crack in the door, the voice asked, "Who sent you?"

"Are you Father Bruno?" Laibale asked, his voice beginning to shake. He was afraid to offer information, since he could not see who he was speaking with.

"What do you want?" the man asked, still standing behind the barely open door.

Laibale took a deep breath and decided to answer truthfully.

"Father John said you might help. My mother is very sick."

"Come in," the voice said quietly as the door widened.

Once inside, the moonlight revealed a smallish man dressed in a pair of trousers and a light sweater. Laibale noticed that he was wearing glasses but no priest's collar.

"You cannot stay here," the man said, lowering his voice more and speaking into Laibale's ear. "There is a group of partisans in the forest, not too far away. They have a doctor with them."

Within minutes, Laibale had thanked him and left the house, buoyed with the knowledge that he might be able to save his mother after all. Father Bruno said the doctor was known for his compassion. He had survived the burning of the hospital at Kovno Ghetto and had only recently escaped the ghetto to join the partisans.

Laibale quickly returned to his mother, excited to tell her the news. Once they were outside, though, his excitement quickly faded when the motorcycle failed to start. No amount of coaxing would bring it to life.

"Mama, we've got to walk for help," Laibale said, trying to sound confident.

"I don't know how much I can walk," his mother replied. The exhaustion had overtaken her.

"Hold on to me. I'll help you." Laibale tried to boost her determination. "We can do this together."

"Just let me die here, Laibale. Save yourself," his mother replied weakly.

"Nonsense! We'll be fine. Here, take my arm."

Fear fed Laibale's rising adrenaline, giving him extra strength. The time to save his mother's life was running out. If they stayed she would surely die. Together they started down the road. They hadn't made it very far before her knees buckled and she sank to the ground. Laibale sat beside her and cradled her head on his lap, expecting her to completely give up. He sat there for a long while, hoping the rest would revive her. Instead, he heard a noise a distance away. Slowly, a farmer's wagon came into view.

"Get up, Mama. Maybe this farmer will give us a ride for a little way."

"You don't know who it is," his mother replied, fear rising in her voice.

"We have to take the chance, Mama."

The wagon drew near and a middle-aged, mustachioed man leaned down.

"Are you having trouble, young fellow?" the man asked.

"Yes, my motorcycle has run out of gas. My mother is sick and we're trying to get to a doctor."

"Get in. I'll give you a lift."

"That's very kind of you, mister," Laibale said. He steadied his mother as she reached for the farmer's hands.

"Well, I'm new here," the man replied. "Might need some help myself one day. I'm headed to the next town. Where's your doctor?"

"Not too far from there," Laibale answered.

"Well, that's lucky."

Laibale helped his mother get comfortable inside the wagon bed where she collapsed with relief. The man struck up a conversation. He told Laibale that he had just moved back into the area, and that his father needed his help on the farm.

"Your mother looks pretty spent. We'll go into town and get some things my father needs and then I'll take you to the doctor."

Laibale's heart sped up thinking of the town. He had heard that all the Jews there had been rounded up and executed just before the ghetto was formed. Laibale was terrified to go into town but he couldn't argue. Instead, he decided to stay quiet and try to think of an alternate plan.

25

Unable To Hide

As they approached the town, Laibale's heart pounded even harder. He wondered what he could do to appear inconspicuous. Finally, he decided he would just stand beside the wagon and talk with his mother. She would, after all, be feeling the same fears. Perhaps more.

The farmer hitched the wagon and strode into the store to make his purchases. Laibale stood close to the wheel, his head tucked down as much as possible, making small talk with his mother. They both tried to appear confident but Laibale knew they didn't. Even though Laibale detested wearing hats, he suddenly wished for one. Within a few minutes, the farmer came back to the doorway.

"Say, boy, can you give me a hand loading this feed?" he asked.

Afraid to do so but unable to refuse, Laibale lowered his head even more and closely followed the man into the store and grabbed the opposite end of one of the sacks. They made three trips to the wagon, carrying sacks of cattle feed and then corn for the chickens. They had picked up the final sack when a boy ran into the store, almost hitting Laibale with the screen door as he entered. Laibale couldn't turn or hide his face without dropping the feed.

"Say, aren't you the Jew boy who won that motorcycle race?" the youth asked.

"Why, no. You must be mistaken," he replied. Laibale tried to sound nonchalant. "I don't live around here." Laibale tried to turn his head and backed out the door. His face reddened as he struggled to hold up his end of the sack.

"You're a liar. You've got the same big ears." The boy followed Laibale outside.

"Jew boy! Jew boy! Big ears! Big ears!"

Laibale managed to hold onto the feed sack until they got it into the wagon. The farmer turned, confused at the confrontation. As the loud taunts continued, a crowd of other boys gathered in a cluster. One of them threw a clod of dirt, hitting Laibale in the face.

"What did you do that for?" the farmer asked nervously, moving to stand between Laibale and the threatening youths who were all bigger than Laibale.

"What's all the commotion?" a man asked, stepping outside the store, pushing himself through the crowd that was forming.

"Pa, ain't this the Jew boy that won that motorcycle race in Kaunas a while back?"

The man walked around Laibale and stared.

"He sure is, son. I'd recognize those ears anywhere." He turned to the farmer. "What do you mean bringing Jews into this town, stranger?"

"I don't know nobody here," the farmer replied. "The boy said his mother was sick and I was just doing them a favor."

"You did them a favor all right," he said, laughing. He looked over his shoulder at the other men who had started gathering. He stepped back inside his store.

The farmer brushed Laibale aside, his friendliness gone.

"Get that Jew out of my wagon. He began pulling on Laibale's mother's arm.

"Leave her be," Laibale said angrily. "I'll get her out."

"Well, be quick about it," another man taunted from the crowd. "We don't want no Jews in this town."

"Yeah," another man added from the growing throng. "We got rid of our Jews once."

Laibale's mother struggled to climb out of the wagon. Just as Laibale helped her right herself, the door to the store slammed. The owner had returned with his shotgun.

"My God, Laibale, he's going to shoot us," his mother said, her knees giving way beneath her.

The stranger pulled her upright again.

"Don't you touch her," Laibale said, his voice turning to ice. The man immediately stepped back.

"Go ahead, Jew boy," the man said, pointing the gun at them. "You and the old woman take your clothes off and leave them. Start walking toward those woods over there."

Laibale turned his back to Nese, trying to spare her dignity, then he began walking, half carrying his mother, followed by a crowd of men, some now hoisting pitchforks and axes. They all shouted insults.

"I'm so sorry, Mama," Laibale whispered, on the verge of tears. "I'm so sorry. If only I hadn't won that race."

"Don't say that," Laibale," his mother replied. "I'm so proud you won that race. No one in Kaunas will ever forget it. Maybe all of Lithuania. As for everything else, you did the best you could do. Remember how you got my medicine and how much it helped me?"

"Yes, I remember, but it wasn't good enough."

"Of course it was good enough," his mother said. She drew herself up taller and walked more steadily. "I'm walking because of it." Her resolve only lasted a few steps before she stumbled. Laibale reached for her again. He increased his hold on her waist, now nearly carrying her. They made their way toward the patch of woods in silence, the distance between them and the men behind them growing greater. They could barely hear the shouting now.

With each step Laibale thought of what he had tried to do. His life before the ghetto seemed light years away. He thought of how much he loved the first snows and the cold winters in Lithuania. That made him smile, thinking of how much he had enjoyed coming home at night to a warm kitchen and his mother's delicious *lochen kugel*.

They got closer to the edge of the woods. The ghetto, the forced labor, even the times he had managed to fool the Nazis seemed a lifetime away. All he could think of was what he would leave behind. He wondered about his brothers and hoped they would live. He wondered if Father John or Father Bruno would be questioned about his and his mother's escape. He regretted not thanking Peter for taking such risks for him. He thought of how Rebekkah had kissed him, recalling the warmth of her cheek on his. Would she marry in the United States and have children? Would she remember him when she saw a motorcycle? Thinking of his motorcycle made him smile a little again. It reminded him of the race day, when he felt like he had conquered the world and had so much to live for. He wondered if any of that mattered now or if anyone would remember him at all.

As if she read his mind, Laibale's mother stood more erect and put her arm around his waist, drawing him even closer to her. "Think of Sara, Little Lion," she said softly. She will live because of you. I just know she will."

The woods exploded with birds as the shots rang out.

Author's Note

The city of Kaunas, often called Kovno, had a suburb known as Slobodka, which was an impoverished area where poor Jews had always lived in Lithuania. Other, richer Jews lived throughout Kaunas. When the Nazis created Kovno Ghetto on August 15, 1941, their Judaism made them all classless. The ghetto, surrounded by barbed wire and guarded, would eventually become home to some 30,000 to 35,000 Jews from Kaunas and the towns nearby. There were no sanitation facilities. Water was provided by four wells and electricity was only available on a sporadic basis. The Jewish menial laborers, who never bothered anybody but stayed to themselves and their plight, suddenly had former millionaires for neighbors.

While *The Little Lion* is a novel, the entire book was historically set in Kovno Ghetto in Kaunas, Lithuania. Many of the events recreated in the book are true. Near the end of the war, Kovno Ghetto was turned into Kauen Concentration Camp 4. Jews from other countries were transported to the camp expressly for extermination. Before fleeing from the incoming Russian military in July 1944, German soldiers burned the ghetto to the ground, killing most of the remaining inmates. Some 40,000 individuals who either lived in the ghetto or were transported there met their death before the war ended. The vast majority were Jews. Approximately 6 percent of the 240,000 Jews living in Lithuania prior to the war survived the Holocaust.

Prior to the ghetto's formation, Laibale Gillman lived with his mother, Nese. His parents were divorced. His oldest brother, Moshe, had a wife named Sheina. Their daughter was named Sara. Israel, the middle brother, had a girlfriend, also named Sheina. In *The Little Lion*, she was called Lola, to avoid confusion. The older Jews, including Laibale, his mother, brothers, and their mates, were among those forced to work as slaves for the Nazis for approximately two years prior to their escape.

Laibale, who proved especially valuable to the Nazis

because of his mechanical expertise of motorcycles, managed to find an escape route. Through trial and error, he came and went, until he developed a plan for the whole family to get through the barbed wire fence that surrounded the ghetto.

Prior to their leaving, Laibale had also orchestrated a way to smuggle Sara, his niece, to a Gentile couple outside the ghetto. She was reunited with her parents after the war. Laibale first led the way for his brothers and their mates to find safely at a nearby farm. He and his mother escaped from the ghetto a short while later but were intercepted and shot by local townspeople on April 26, 1944. A farmer, who had previously befriended the Gillmans, told Israel and Moshe about the deaths and also where the bodies could be found. A burial was arranged after the war. Israel Gillman had the remains exhumed and reinterred in Israel in 1982.

Epilogue

Israel and Sheina Gillman moved to Germany in 1945, where a daughter, Etty, was born. They moved to Israel in 1949 where Erit, another daughter, was born. The Gillman family moved to Canada in 1953 where Mr. Gillman established a successful hosiery manufacturing plant. He is retired. Sheina Gillman died in 2014.

Israel and Sheina Gillman have three grandsons and one granddaughter, as well as four great-grandsons and two great-granddaughters. All of the Gillmans and their descendants live in Canada and/or the United States.

~~~~

Moshe, Sheina, and Sara Gillman remained in Lithuania where another daughter, Liuba, and a son, David, were born. Mr. and Mrs. Gillman and several family members moved to Israel in 1971 and later to Canada.

Sara Gillman pursued a medical degree in Lithuania and married Joseph Pliamm. They and their son, Lew (who was named for Laibale Gillman), moved to Israel in 1972. The family subsequently moved to Canada where a daughter, Naomi, was born. Since 1979, the Gillmans and all their descendants have lived in Canada, where Dr. Pliamm maintains a general practice. Both of her children are also physicians. She and her husband have five grandchildren. While she doesn't remember her Uncle Laibale, she acknowledges that he saved her life and refers to him as her hero. She does vividly remember reuniting with her parents, recognizing the red dress with white polka dots her mother was wearing at the time.

Moshe and Sheina Gillman have four grandsons, two granddaughters, four great grandsons and four great-granddaughters. Moshe Gillman died in 1993. Sheina Gillman died in 2011.

~~~~

Meck, known only by his first name, was hanged in Kovno Ghetto. His mother and sister were later executed at Fort IX.

~~~~

Dr. Elchanan Elkes, who served tirelessly as the chairman of the Jewish Council in Kovno Ghetto, risking his life to save so many others, was transported to Landsberg concentration camp in Germany, and put in charge of the camp's hospital hut. Elkes became ill there and died on October 17, 1944. His wife, Miriam, survived the war. Their two children, Joel and Sarah, who were not in Lithuania during the war, became physicians.

~~~~

Chaim Yellin, an inmate at Kovno Ghetto who escaped to aid the partisans' fight against the Nazis, was killed prior to the end of WWII. There are conflicting reports of how he died.

~~~~

Master Sergeant Helmut Rauca fled to Canada after the war. He was extradited to Frankfurt, Germany, in 1983, when it was determined that he lied on his immigration documents, nullifying his Canadian citizenship. He was charged with aiding and abetting in the murder of more than 11,500 persons between 1941 and 1943 in Kaunas, Lithuania. Rauca died in Germany before being brought to trial.

~~~~

In May 1997, the Virginia Holocaust Museum was established on Roseneath Road in Richmond, Va., in a former education building of Temple Beth-El. The museum contains exhibits that pertain to many aspects of the Holocaust, including some depicting the Gillman family, as well as other Jewish Lithuanian families. The museum was moved to a new location, 2000 E. Cary Street, provided by the Virginia General Assembly and was dedicated during a Yom HaShoah memorial service in April 2003.

Sheina Gillman (circa 1978)

Courtesy Israel Gillman

Israel Gillman (date unknown)

Courtesy Israel Gillman

Israel Gillman, with daughters Erit (L) and Etty(R) (circa 1982)

Courtesy Israel Gillman

Reinterment of Nese and Laibale Gillman from Lithuania to Tel Aviv. Man at far right is Israel Gillman (1982)

Gravesite at Tel Aviv, Israel. (1982)

Neil Bienstock and Israel Gillman. Grandson and grandfather celebrate Mr. Gillman's 94th birthday (2015)

Laibale Gillman (Passport photo 1939)

Nese Gillman (Passport photo 1939)

Courtesy Dr. Sara Gillman Pliamm

Sara Gillman as a child, with Ona and Jonas Valcekauskas, one of the Gentile couples who harbored her during the Holocaust (1944)

Courtesy Sheina Gillman and Dr. Sara Pliamm

(left to right) Sheina, Sara, Liuba and Moshe Gillman (circa 1949).

Nomeda Repsytė (right) and Virginia Vasiliauskienė Mann provided invaluable guidance, knowledge, and expertise to the author during several of her trips to Lithuania. Mrs. Mann's grandparents, mother, and uncle helped save eight Jews who escaped from Kovno Ghetto. All four of them were declared Righteous Among the Nations by Yad Vashem. One of the survivors, Henry Kellen, helped establish the El Paso Holocaust Museum in Texas. (2009)

The author and Dr. Irena Veisaitė, while visiting in the latter's home in Vilnius. A Kovno Ghetto survivor, Professor Veisaitė earned her doctorate in Leningrad. She was a lecturer at the Pedagogical University in Vilnius, Lithuania (1953-1997). She was active in creating and leading the Thomas Mann Cultural Centre and also the Open Society Fund in Lithuania. In 2012, she was awarded the Goethe Medal for her contribution to the cultural exchange between Germany and Lithuania. Known for addressing the Holocaust and the Soviet occupation of her country, she reflects on the communist times in Lithuania by saying, "The Soviets were very bad. Different from the Nazis, but not better." (2010)

Fort IX, also known as the Ninth Fort, has been turned into a museum (2009)

Ninth Fort Monument by A. Ambraziunas (2009)

Simonas Dovidavičius, director of the Sugihara Museum in Kaunas, Lithuania, tells the author about the route that many Jews took to safely by using one of the Sugihara fake passports. (2010)

Courtesy Nancy Wright Beasley

Chiune Sugihara (1900-1986) was Vice Consul for the Japanese Empire in Kaunas, Lithuania from 1939 to 1940. He risked his career and his family's safety to provide visas that helped facilitate the escape, and probably near-certain death of over 6,000 Jews to Japanese territory. As a result, he was disgraced in Japan and removed from diplomatic service. The consulate building where he worked in Kaunas is now a museum. He has been declared Righteous Among the Nations by Yad Vashem. (2010)

Courtesy Nancy Wright Beasley

Anne E. Derse (front left), U. S. ambassador to Lithuania, sits beside the author and listens to comments following a book presentation at the ambassador's home. (2010)

Anne E. Derse, U. S. ambassador to Lithuania, with the author and Samuel Bak, a survivor of the Vilna Ghetto in Lithuania and a well-known Holocaust artist. (2010)

Book Club Questions

1. Did you enjoy the book? Why? Why not?

2. What about the plot? Was it believable? Did it pull you in; or did you feel you had to force yourself to read the book?

3. How realistic was the characterization? Would you want to meet any of the characters? Which characters do you particularly admire or dislike?

4. Did the actions of the characters seem plausible? Why? Why not?

5. What motivates a given character's actions? Do you think those actions are justified or ethical?

6. If one (or more) of the characters made a choice that had moral implications, would you have made the same decision? Why? Why not?

7. Do any characters grow or change during the course of the novel? If so, in what way?

8. Who in this book would you most like to meet? What would you ask — or say?

9. If you could insert yourself as a character in the book, what role would you play?

10. What are some of the book's themes?

11. Did the book end the way you expected? Why? Why not?

12. Would you recommend this book to other readers? To your close friend?

13. If you were to talk with the author, what would you want to know?

Standards of Learning/Virginia

English
5.1, 5.2, 5.3, 5.5, 6.1, 6.2, 6.3, 6.5, 7.1, 7.3, 7.5, 7.6, 8.1, 8.2, 8.3, 8.5, 8.6, 9.2, 9.3, 9.4, 9.5, 9.8, 10.1, 10.2, 10.4, 10.5, 10.8, 11.2, 11.5, 12.2, 12.5

History and Social Science
WHII.11, WHII.12, WHII.13, WHII.15, VUS.11, VUS.12

Theatre Arts
6.1, 6.2, 6.3, 6.7, 6.8, 6.11, 6.15, 6.22, 6.23

7.1, 7.2, 7.3, 7.5, 7.9, 7.13, 7.17, 7.19

8.1, 8.2, 8.3, 8.4, 8.10, 8.11, 8.16, 8.21, 8.25

TI.2, TI.3, TI.4, TI.8, TI.9, TI.10, TI.12, TI.18

TII.2, TII.4, TII.5, TII.10, TII.11, TII.12, TII.13, TII.15, TII.16, TII.17, TII.21

TIII.2, TIII.3, TIII.4, TIII.5, TIII.7, TIII .8, TIII.9, TIII.13, TIII.16, TIII.19

TIV.1, TIV.2, TIV.4, TIV.6, TIV.7, TIV.9, TIV.11, TIV.12, TIV.13, TIV.17, TIV.18

Activities

1. Verbal/Linguistics

a. Write a poem.

b. Design a crossword puzzle using key words from the story. The definitions should show the importance of the words.

2. Logical/Mathematical

a. Design a Time Line including all of the major events in the story.

b. Create a chart to analyze the similarities and differences in *The Little Lion* and another Holocaust story you have read. Consider characters, location, hiding places, capture, imprisonment, and protectors. Use at least 10 similarities and 10 differences.

c. Create a chart to analyze the causes and effects of the events in the story.

3. Visual/Spatial

a. Draw pictures that depict a summary of the most important events in the story. Write a caption that explains the significance of the drawing for each picture.

b. Design a memorial/monument for the Holocaust relating to the events in the story. Write an explanation to accompany your work.

c. Create a Liberation Camp for Holocaust /war survivors.

d. Illustrate the most significant event in *The Little Lion* that touched you. Write a supporting description.

4. Theatre/Technology/Video

a. Act out a scene in the book using the characters of Laibale and/or his brothers. Write a paragraph(s) explaining the development of the event you have chosen to perform.

b. Design a memorial/monument for the Holocaust relating to the events in the story. Write a summary to accompany your work.

c. In groups, choose one of the following: 1.) Create a short script based on a scene in the book, use video to record the scene, and use available editing software to edit and present your scene to the class. 2.) Choose a theme, moral, or lesson from the story. Create a new story relevant to your life now that connect to this theme, moral, or lesson. Write a short script. Film the scene. Edit on available editing software and present to your class. 3.) Create a script as a documentary (documenting events in a scene as real-life events). Edit on available software.

Activities

5. Musical/Rhythmic

a. Compose a song (instrumental or with words) describing one or more specific events in the story. You may tape the performance in class. Write a paragraph(s) explaining which event(s) you chose and an interpretation of the music.

b. Create a song with words to highlight the important points of the story, choosing dominant facts/events.

6. Interpersonal

a. Write a letter of encouragement to Laibale while he is in the ghetto or in hiding.

b. Plan at least 3 strategies for a variety of people to get along in hiding or in a ghetto. Write a description explaining in detail how to implement the plan.

c. Interview a veteran/liberator (or survivor of a war). Prepare interview questions for teacher to review in advance.

d. Create a Liberation Camp for Holocaust/war survivors. (See #7c, "Naturalist")

e. Evaluate the personal strengths and weaknesses of Laibale. Write specific, vivid examples and details. Did Laibale's actions influence your beliefs/thoughts regarding discrimination and/or bullying?

f. Write about a personal struggle you have experienced. Explain the problem, how you overcame it, and what lesson(s) you have learned.

7. Naturalist

a. If you were in hiding, what would you miss most about the natural world (i.e., plants, animals, weather). Do NOT cite mechanical, technological, material, etc. Explain why you would miss those things. Explain how you would compensate for those missing elements in your life (What would you use or do to replace those elements.)

b. Design a model of some part of Kovno Ghetto, such as the guard gate where slave laborers had to pass inspection, either going to or returning from work. Write a paragraph(s) explaining each part of the display and the specific difficulties and challenges endured.

c. Design a model of a Liberation Camp for Holocaust war survivors. Write a paragraph(s) explaining the purpose of each area of the camp and how the design might help with healing.

Recommended Resources

Between Shades of Gray by Ruta Sepetys

Briar Rose by Jane Yolen

From a Name to a Number by Alter Wiener

Hidden History of the Kovno Ghetto, United States Holocaust Memorial Museum, edited by Dennis Klein

Hitler's Youth by Susan Campbell Bartoletti

If I Should Die Before I Wake by Han Nolan

Izzy's Fire: Finding Humanity in the Holocaust by Nancy Wright Beasley

Milkweed by Jerry Spinelli

Number the Stars by Lois Lowry

Run, Boy, Run by Uri Orlev

Sarah's Key by Tatiana de Rosnay

Secret of Gabi's Dresser by Kathy Kacer

Smuggled in Potato Sacks – Fifty Stories of the Hidden Children of the Kaunas Ghetto, Editors: Solomon Abramovich and Yakov Zilbert

Surviving the Holocaust: The Kovno Ghetto Diary by Avraham Tory, edited by Martin Gilbert

The Book Thief by Markus Zusak

The Boy Who Dared by Susan Campbell Bartoletti

The Complete Maus (Maus, #1-2) by Art Spiegelman

The Guernsey Literary and Potato Peel Pie Society by Mary Ann Shaffer

The Hiding Place by Corrie ten Boom

The Holocaust: The Human Tragedy by Martin Gilbert

The Pianist: The Extraordinary Story of One Man's Survival in Warsaw, 1939-45 by Wladyslaw Szpilman

The Routledge Atlas of the Holocaust by Martin Gilbert

The Underground Reporters by Kathy Kacer

The World Must Know: The History of the Holocaust as Told in the United States Holocaust Memorial Museum by Michael Berenbaum

We Are Here: Memories of the Lithuanian Holocaust by Ellen Cassedy

About the Author

Nancy Wright Beasley started her journalistic career as a state correspondent for *The Richmond New Leader* in 1979, while she and her family lived in South Hill, Va. After her husband's death in 1991, she settled in Richmond, Va., launching a freelance career. She wrote for several publications while also serving as a personal columnist and contributing editor for *Richmond* magazine from 1998 through 2014.

Photo by Jay Paul

In 2005, the Virginia Press Women named Beasley as their Communicator of Achievement, and in 2006, the Richmond YWCA chose her as one of Ten Outstanding Women in Central Virginia. Also in 2006, her book, *Izzy's Fire: Finding Humanity in the Holocaust*, was nominated for a People's Choice Award, a competition sponsored by the James River Writers and the Library of Virginia. The book also won first-place awards in the historical books category in competition through the Virginia Press Women and the National Federation of Press Women. It has been consistently taught in schools and universities in the United States and can be found in public and private libraries in several countries. In 2015 Beasley was the featured author at the Fifth Annual Virginia Commonwealth University Alumni's Monroe Scholars Book and Author luncheon that raised more than $8,000 for student scholarships.

A member of Brandermill Rotary Club (Midlothian, Va.), Beasley has offered presentations at a variety of clubs, including the Kaunas Rotary Club in Lithuania and the Jerusalem Rotary Club in Israel. She has also spoken at numerous schools and institutions, including Yale University, as well as at Siauilai University and Vytautas Magnus University, both located in Lithuania. *Izzy's Fire* is used in numerous Holocaust education courses in schools and universities.

A second nonfiction book, *Reflections of a Purple Zebra: Essays of a Different Stripe*, a compilation of Beasley's personal columns from *Richmond* magazine, was published in 2007.

In 2000, Beasley earned a master's degree in the School of Mass Communications at Virginia Commonwealth University and taught there as an adjunct professor from 2000 through 2003. She completed a master of fine arts in children's literature in 2011 at Hollins University in Roanoke, Va., made possible through the generosity of Neil November, a Richmond philanthropist and ardent patron of the arts. Stage rights for her thesis, *The Little Lion*, were obtained by Swift Creek Mill Theatre. The play adaptation, written by playwright Irene Ziegler, and directed by Tom Width, was presented on stage during the Mill's 50th anniversary season in 2016.

www.nancywrightbeasley.com   nancy@nancywrightbeasley.com